Vlad the Inhaler

Hero in the Making

Lorraine Mace

Incredible Books 2017

Join Vlad on facebook:
www.facebook.com/IamVladTheInhaler/

This book is dedicated with much love to my grandsons, Tégan, Reeve and Jacob.

Contents

Chapter One

Half Bred, Fully Miserable

Vlad had never known such hunger. Weak with longing, he was driven insane by the smell of the ripe flesh he held in his shaking hands. He let his fangs pierce the soft downy skin and sank to his knees. Nothing had ever tasted as wonderful as this; knowing it was forbidden added to the sensation. He closed his eyes and bit deeper, filling his mouth with the sweet fluid.

The bedroom door flew open, hitting the stone wall with such force windows rattled, spiders scuttled back to their cobwebs and half the candles blew out.

Aunt Valentyna towered above him, red eyes glaring, jet black hair standing on end, and ruby lips curled into a snarl.

"I knew it!" she thundered. "I knew you were doing something disgusting. What exactly are you eating, you repulsive excuse for a child?"

Vlad choked and dropped his feast, splattering flesh on the flagstone floor.

"Well, I'm waiting. What is that?" his aunt demanded, touching the half-eaten peach with the pointed toe of her shoe before reaching down to pick it up.

Vlad could feel the juice dripping from his chin and wished he'd eaten faster. His stomach ached. In the last four days he'd only had an apple and a banana. The peach was the last of his human food. He flinched as she grabbed him by the collar. Although he kicked and wriggled, she lifted him with one hand as if he weighed no more than a bat's wing.

"Can't fly, can't drink blood, and can't even breathe half the time. No wonder your parents hid you away. Imagine the disgrace of bringing a hupyre into the family. What a pathetic specimen you are. I'd have had you put down at birth." She threw the remains of the peach out of the window. "Well, you disgusting half-breed, what was that revolting object?"

Vlad tried to answer, but it felt as though someone had stuffed cotton wool down his

throat. He couldn't drag his ey
points of her fangs. Tears of fr
down his face. Gasping, he tried aga..

"P ... p ... p ..."

"What? What did you say?"

"P ... p ... peach."

"Disgusting," she said, and flung him across the room.

Thudding against his bed, he scrambled round to face her. Looking up at his furious aunt, he tried to control his wheezing. Desperately, he struggled to breathe out. His mouth opened and closed, but he couldn't drag any air into his swollen lungs. The more he panicked, the harder it was to breathe.

"Stop making that pathetic noise, right now! How many times do I have to tell you that vampires don't get asthma? Where did you get that ... that thing?" she demanded. "If it was one of the servants ..."

Valentyna left the sentence unfinished, but Vlad knew what she meant and shivered. The last servant who'd tried to help him had joined the family for a feast. As the main course.

"C ... c ... cupboard. Hid ... fruit ... there."

She yanked open the wardrobe door and dragged everything out. Clothes flew across

.ıe room and landed in a heap on the floor.

"If I find so much as a mouldy grape, out the window it goes, and you'll go with it. A disgrace to the vampire heritage, that's what you are. What's wrong with normal food?" she scolded, snatching up the glass of congealed blood from his bedside table.

As she waved it under his nose the thick sludge broke through the skin that had formed on top and Vlad's stomach heaved.

"You've let this get cold. What a waste of fine food. I'm going to bring some fresh blood and stand over you until every drop has gone."

She raised her hand and leant forward, sneering. Her long, curved incisors gleamed in the candlelight. Vlad shrank back, hands over his head waiting for the slap. But it didn't come. Valentyna laughed and slammed the door as she left.

He heard the key turn in the lock and staggered breathless to the window. Leaning out, he felt behind the drainpipe, reaching for his inhaler. He fumbled, almost dropping it in his desperate need to get it into his mouth. He pressed the button and glorious air filled his tortured lungs. Closing his eyes, he leant against the window ledge. He was exhausted from the attack, but now felt only relief. Pure relief.

When he opened his eyes again, a sense of desperation made him feel sick. He couldn't take much more of Valentyna's bullying – and he certainly couldn't face another glass of blood. He had to escape, but how?

If only he could master turning into a bat, he could fly away. He stared out of the window. The castle was perched on the edge of a sheer cliff. Far below, waves crashed onto vicious jagged rocks. Bright moonlight glinted on the water. He leant out as far as he could and strained his body to the right so that he could see the edge of Dank Forest. The castle stood in a clearing, surrounded by the forest stretching away as far as the eye could see to the front and the sides. Dark and brooding, that was the last place he should go, even if he could somehow climb down and swim over to the shore without being swept onto the rocks. The forest was home to the most deadly enemies known to vampires – werewolves!

Think. He had to think. There must be a way to get away from the castle. But even if he did, where would he go? He had the ocean in front of him and werewolves on land. He fought off the urge to cry. You're eleven, not a baby, he told himself. He replaced his precious inhaler in its hiding place and turned back into the room.

Hanging over the fireplace was the new coat of arms Valentyna had ordered to be placed in every room in the castle. The two intertwined Vs for Viktor and Valentyna pointed down like fangs. Ruby blood dripped into a pool below.

Apart from the new crest, his room still looked the same as it had before his aunt and her family arrived. He loved this room. If only he could keep his family out and find some food, he'd feel safe in it. The springy mobile of rubber bats still hung above his oak four-poster bed, as it had since he'd been a baby. Posters of his favourite bands covered most of the walls and ceiling. Nightstar and the Screamers shared space with The Grateful Undead.

He went to the dresser and picked up his parents' wedding photo. His mother looked beautiful in white lace, smiling up at the black empty space where his father stood. Not having a reflection messed up family pictures, but Vlad was sure his dad must have looked handsome on his wedding day.

Vlad looked very like his dad apart from the colour of his hair. His formed a widow's peak, just like a normal vampire, but was the colour of straw. He had the same pointed chin and button nose as his dad, but he had his mother's blue eyes.

He gazed at the photograph.

"Where are you?" he whispered. "I don't believe you're dead. I'd feel it, I'm sure I would. But where are you?"

He sat on his bed, staring at the picture, and thought back to the last time he'd seen them – the same day his new relatives had arrived.

* * *

"Vlad, Daddy and I are going out for a walk in the moonlight. Would you like to come with us?" his mother asked.

Vlad grunted and shook his head, concentrating on his game of *Bats and Belfries* with his old nurse.

"Uh, uh, I've almost taken over the castle and Mary will have to surrender."

He glanced up at his mother and blew her a kiss. Ilya, his magnificent father, the Count of Malign, grinned.

"Total domination, eh, Vlad?"

Vlad showed him his cards. Three pitchforks, a coffin and two jugs of holy water.

"Mary, my dear, I think he's right. Unless you get some very lucky throws of the dice, you're going to lose."

"I've never won yet, sir. The young master is too good for me."

Vlad waved his mum and dad off, then shook the dice box and grinned.

"Now you're in for it, Mary. Prepare to get wiped out."

An hour later Vlad had won his game. He didn't expect his parents back for ages and it was when he was alone like this that he most wished he had a friend. Stuck between two species was a rotten place to be. He didn't fit in anywhere. He loved Mary and knew she loved him, but he wondered what it would be like to have a friend his own age.

He decided to pass the time trying to turn into a bat. Surely this time he'd be able to do it. Maybe it was because he was half-human, but he'd never yet got it right. His dad could transform instantly, and Vlad had often watched with envy as he'd soared across the night sky. He concentrated as hard as he could, but nothing happened. Then, just when he was almost sure he could feel his body changing, his bedroom door crashed open.

Four smiling strangers stood in the doorway. From their teeth he knew they were vampires, either that, or their dentist had gone mad with a sharpening tool.

"Who are you?" he asked.

The man could have been his father's twin, they were so alike. He had the same handsome features and black sweptback hair. The difference was in the smile, this man's grin was hideous. Holding his arm was a woman with red-rimmed eyes and hair the colour of a raven's wing.

"He's too skinny. Not a very healthy-looking child," she said to the tall, muscular boy standing by her side.

"He looks like a puny human with those weird blue eyes," the boy said. "And he's got funny coloured hair. Yuck."

"Why aren't you dressed properly?" the woman asked.

"I am," Vlad said. He looked down at his jeans, sweatshirt and trainers and couldn't understand what she meant. Then he realised – they were all in traditional vampire evening dress.

Leaning against the doorframe was the smallest of the four; the most beautiful girl Vlad had ever seen. Silken black hair framed a white face, eyes of coal gleamed, and her lips were like a perfect rose. When she smiled, Vlad's heart seemed to leave his body, fly five times round the room and land back in his narrow chest with a sickening thud.

The man spoke at last. "Who are we? Why, Vladimir, we are your family. We've come to take care of you, haven't we, Valentyna?"

The woman nodded, lifted off the floor and floated across to Vlad. He shrank away and clattered into a chair.

"Are you frightened, little one? How amusing! Meet your cousins. Boris, Gretchen, say hello to Vladimir."

Vlad stared at his beautiful cousin. He wished he could look at her forever.

"Can we kill him now?" she asked.

Vlad's already unsteady heart almost stopped beating. With a thump, he fell out of love. Swaying, he clutched the back of the chair.

"No, Gretchen," said Valentyna, "vampires don't kill other vampires, not even half-species like your hupyre cousin; besides, we need him to deal with the lawyer."

"What have you done with my mum and dad? Where are they?"

"So sad," the man said, "but the villagers attacked and killed your parents this evening. I'm Viktor, your father's younger brother."

Stunned, Vlad slumped back onto his bed.

"What? They can't have. That can't be true. Why would the villagers do that?"

"Ilya, your late and very irritating father, killed a child in the village," Viktor said.

"He would never do that," Vlad screamed. "Dad gave up drinking blood when he married my mum. You're lying."

At that moment, Barton the butler forced his way into the room.

"What's going on here? Who are you people? I think you'd better leave before my master and mistress get back."

"Mr Barton," Vlad pleaded, "they say my mum and dad are dead. They say they've come to live here."

"Barton, what a charming name," Valentyna said, running her hands over the butler's plump quivering form like a butcher at a cattle market. "Would you care to join us for dinner? There's more than enough of you to go round."

The four vampires moved as one towards the butler. Vlad ran and blocked their way.

"Leave him alone. He's my friend," he shouted.

"Oh goody," said Valentyna. "It's always nice to have friends for dinner." She grabbed Vlad's arm and held him. "You get second bite," she said and sank her fangs into the butler's neck.

Vlad tried to pull away, but Valentyna held him fast. When she'd finished drinking, she lifted him and shoved his face into Mr Barton's bloody neck.

"I won't," he said, but his mouth filled with warm blood.

He couldn't breathe. He gasped, desperate to get air into his lungs, but each gasp sucked more blood into his mouth. Sickened by the taste, he tried to spit it out, but his need for air stopped him. Spitting and sucking, he choked.

"Look, Mama, he can't breathe," yelled Boris.

Valentyna let him go and Vlad hit the floor with a thud.

"Your great-great-great-great-great-grandfather,

Vlad the Impaler, would be ashamed of you," she sneered.

Vlad tried not to be sick as he reached inside his pocket for his inhaler. He shoved it in his mouth and sucked.

"Listen to him wheezing and snuffling. He sounds like one of those stupid humans back home. Oh look, he has an inhaler just like they do. Hey, that's an idea, let's call him Vlad the Inhaler," Gretchen said.

Valentyna snatched the inhaler from him.

"Vampires don't get asthma, so you won't need this," she said, throwing it out of the window. "Now, who shall we have as our next course?"

* * *

Vlad had endured so much misery in the week since the family of four had arrived, but at least Valentyna hadn't found his spare inhaler. He'd prayed every night for his mum and dad to come back, but they hadn't. Putting the photo back on his dresser, he lay on his bed, trying to ignore the hunger squeezing his stomach.

He gazed back at the photograph and the

feeling that his parents weren't dead grew even stronger. There was no way they would have left him to face Valentyna and Viktor on his own. So, if they were alive, and he was certain they were, that must mean they were in even worse trouble than him.

He had to come up with a plan to escape and find them. If only he were as big as Boris, but no, he'd have to be bigger, much bigger to fight all of them. A tear fell, but he scrubbed at his face with his sleeve; he wasn't a weakling.

* * *

Valentyna swept through the corridors of Castle Malign, gazing lovingly at the priceless antiques and family portraits. Some of the most vicious vampires in history had owned these treasures. It wasn't right that Vlad's father should have had all this, especially as he hadn't the common decency to be truly evil. She'd grown up in a tiny two-roomed hovel, but she'd always known she was meant to live in a big house with servants. She'd slept with her bedroom window open and her neck on display for months before Viktor finally came to call. It had been worth dying to move so far up the social ladder. She'd worked hard to get rid of her common accent, and now no one would ever know she hadn't been born a lady of delicate tastes. She'd planned and schemed to get rid of Vlad's parents and, finally, it had paid off. Her beloved *aristocratic* husband would inherit everything.

A movement caught her attention. She turned. One of the plumper housemaid blood-banks cowered behind a curtain. Valentyna carried on, resisting temptation. It really was time for her to diet; she'd only drink from skinny people from now on.

Yes, Viktor would be a worthy successor to his mighty ancestor. Vlad the Impaler would be turning in his coffin at the thought of a wheezy hupyre ruling Magdorovia. Well, he would be, if angry peasants hadn't set fire to the coffin several hundred years earlier.

Her pleasant night-dreams were interrupted by the sight of her son dangling a screaming housemaid over the balcony.

"Boris, how many times must I tell you not to play with your food?"

"Sorry, Mama."

The housemaid hit the ground with a splat.

Valentyna shuddered. They'd never get the bloodstains out of the flagstones. She couldn't help but compare Boris with his puny cousin. Boris' vampire skills were the equal of his father's, unlike the half-human monstrosity who'd never killed anyone. The shame of it – a hupyre in such a noble family! She blamed ex-Count Ilya, he should have known better than to leave his wife as an unbitten human.

"Mama, Papa is waiting for you in the library. There's a frightened human in there with him. Do you think it's the lawyer?"

"Oh, I do hope so, Boris. Once we find out where the treasure is hidden we can throw your disgraceful cousin to the werewolves. Here, take this glass. Be a good boy and get some fresh blood for Vlad. Find your sister and the two of you can have some fun forcing him to drink it."

Valentyna ran her fingers through his hair as she floated past. Looking up at the massive silver chandeliers glowing with the light of hundreds of candles, she laughed.

"I do love this castle, Boris. I always knew I'd died for something better than a rundown ruin in a nowhere place like Subversia. We are the upper classes. Don't you ever forget it."

* * *

The library was built to magnificent proportions, with books lining the walls from floor to ceiling. An enormous desk dominated one corner and several couches were placed around the room so people could read in comfort. Valentyna didn't think comfort was on Timms' mind. He looked decidedly *un*comfortable – just the way she liked her humans.

Timms Solicitors had served the family as far back in time as records were kept and knew all the Malign secrets. Viktor loomed over the trembling little man. Valentyna shivered with delight. She adored Viktor when he loomed – he did it with such class.

She lounged on the sofa against the wall behind Timms and rustled her silk dress to remind the man that Viktor wasn't his only problem. He had as big a threat behind him as he had in front.

"He doesn't look very tasty, does he, my love?" she said and laughed as Timms twitched, making his briefcase slide from his knee and thump to the floor.

"So, let me make sure I have this right," purred Viktor. "You refuse to tell me the whereabouts of *my* treasure?"

"S … sir, I can only say … that is … if Vlad's father, the Count is, er, dead … I can only … I must inform the boy, Vlad, himself."

"I'm getting bored," Valentyna sighed. "Why not strangle him until he tells you, dearest?"

Viktor's hands snaked towards the trembling lawyer and grabbed him by the collar.

"Arrghhhhhhhhhhh! That burnt! What have you got on your clothes?"

"Um, sorry. Mrs Timms washes my clothes in holy water. For protection, you see. I've, er, I've got garlic in my pockets, too. Um, and a cross under my shirt."

Valentyna leapt from the sofa and shot through the air to Viktor, carefully avoiding contact with the cowering lawyer. Satisfied that Viktor's burn was only slight, she spun round and made a grab for the lawyer's briefcase.

"Er, it isn't in there. It's in my head."

"What is?" Valentyna snapped.

"The verse. It's a verse, you know. The location of the treasure is in, um, verse."

"So if you know where it is, how come you haven't taken it for yourself?"

"And break the *law*? Me, a *law*yer, break the *law*? My goodness me, that would never do. Besides, I don't."

"Don't what?"

"Know."

"Know what?" screeched Valentyna.

"Um, know the location of the treasure. Count Ilya only told me the verse. He said Vlad would be able to work out what it, um, meant."

"So what is the verse?" Valentyna asked, changing tactics and trying a sweet smile.

"In the west wing of the tower, near to all Maligns hold dear … Oh, oh. You nearly had me there."

"Right, you," Valentyna said. "I've had enough of this. We don't hurt those who are useful to us. Are you prepared to be useful and tell Vlad the verse?"

"Yes, oh yes. Oh my goodness me, yes. I will indeed."

"Good. Come with us. Once you've recited the verse you can go."

Timms gathered his papers and briefcase and made for the door. As they walked along the corridor Valentyna inhaled deeply. The best smell in the world was fear, and this little man smelled divine.

* * *

"Master Vlad. Master Vlad."

Vlad sat up, not sure whether he'd heard someone whisper his name. He crept to the door and listened.

"Master Vlad, it's me, Mary. Open up."

"Mary? How did you get in the castle? Go away before they catch you."

"I sneaked in, but never mind that now. Open the door."

"I can't, she locked it."

"That lawyer's arrived to recite the verse your daddy told you about. I'm terrified they'll kill you once they've heard it. I'll see if I can find the spare key in the butler's pantry and be back as quick as can be. Just you hang on."

Vlad heard her footsteps receding and sank to the floor. He sat with his ear pressed against the door, listening for Mary's return. Then he heard voices and footsteps echoing along the stone corridor.

"Don't push, Gretchen. I'll spill the blood."

"Well, hurry up then. I'll twist his arms behind his back and hurt him until he screams. When his mouth is wide open, you can pour the blood down his throat."

Vlad's breath shortened and he felt his chest tighten. Now wasn't the time to have an asthma attack, he had to escape. He ran to the window and snatched his inhaler from its hiding place. If only he could fly. Maybe if he threw himself from the window ledge, he'd learn before he hit the rocks. He looked down at the waves crashing onto the jagged edges far below and went dizzy. Spinning away from the window, he shoved the inhaler in the pocket of his jeans and hunted for cover. The four-poster was a possibility, but none of the other pieces of furniture were large enough to hide him. The bedroom he loved had become his prison.

The sound of the key turning in the lock made up his mind. He ran back to the window and climbed out onto the ledge.

Chapter Two

Life's a Peach and then You Fly

"Greening, Greening!" screeched Mary.

She'd run all the way from the castle to her cottage in the grounds. Her husband wasn't inside, so she rushed out into the garden.

"Oh, drat the man," she fumed, "never around when he's needed. Greeeeeeeeeeeeeeeeeening!"

A shadow, thrown by the full moon's light, appeared from behind a rhododendron.

"Garlic," Mary gasped. "I've got garlic in my pockets. Don't hurt me, don't bite me …"

The shadow moved closer. She tried to run, but fear kept her firmly rooted like one of her husband's potato plants.

"Mary, is that you?"

Relief washed over her trembling body at the sound of Joe's voice.

"You great lummox! What did you go and frighten me like that for?"

"I didn't mean to, Mary. I was in my greenhouse and heard you yelling. I came to see what's wrong."

"We've got to save Master Vlad," Mary gasped. They're going to kill him."

"Who are?"

"The Maligns, you idiot. Who else would I mean? They've had that wittering lawyer in about the treasure. I just know they're going to feed Vlad to the werewolves," Mary said, her voice breaking.

"How do you know? You haven't been up to the castle, have you? You promised me you wouldn't."

"Joe, I had to. Master Vlad needs help."

"That's as maybe, but I don't want you going there again. Now, calm down and …"

"Calm down? *Calm down?* How can I calm down? He's locked in his room. I couldn't find the spare key. They're going to throw him to the werewolves I tell you; I heard that awful woman laughing about it. We've got to *do* something, Joe."

"Don't be daft. There's only the two of us. What can we do?" he asked.

"I've got garlic in the kitchen *and* some holy water. I'll distract them and you rush up and hammer stakes through their hearts," she commanded.

Joe gulped. "Me? You want *me* to hammer bits of wood into people? What, even the twins?"

"Especially the twins," Mary insisted. "They're more vicious than their parents. Right, come on, look lively. We've not got much time."

* * *

Vlad pressed his back against the castle wall as he inched along the narrow ledge. He'd climbed out determined to jump, but now he couldn't bring himself to do it. The howling wind dragged at his clothes, pulling him forwards. Pounding waves crashed off the rocks below. If he fell, he'd better learn to fly before hitting the bottom.

His vampire half probably wouldn't die. Probably. Maybe. Pity the human half might end up squished. He thought about his options and they weren't good. Face Boris and Gretchen, who would force blood down his throat, or jump? Okay, on the count of three, he'd jump.

He mouthed the words. One, two … What would happen if his human half did die, which vampire bits would survive? Better not to think about that, besides, he'd *definitely* fly before hitting the bottom. Probably. How hard could it be? Okay, deep breath. He gasped for air and nearly lost his grip on the stones behind him. Waves of fear and nausea made him lightheaded. Trying to stop his heart from leaping out of his mouth, he got ready again. One, two …

He could hear Boris and Gretchen inside his room. Inching further away from the window, he came up against a drainpipe blocking his way. He clung to the stones and listened.

"Where is the scrawny little freak?"

"I bet he's under the bed, Boris," Gretchen squealed. "Lift the bed. Let's drag him out. Oh, I was sure he'd be there. What about in the wardrobe? Behind the chest of drawers?"

Vlad heard his furniture being dragged about the room; it was only a matter of time before they realised where he was. Maybe he should jump anyway. He looked down. Big mistake. Okay, count to three without looking down.

Boris' voice drifted out. "He must have flown away."

"He can't fly! He tries and tries and just can't," laughed Gretchen.

"Maybe he's hiding outside on the ledge," said Boris.

Vlad took a deep breath.

One!

Two!

Three!

He leapt into the night flapping his arms, but nothing happened. Harder, harder, harder, he flapped, screaming as the rocks rushed up towards him. Suddenly he was yanked sideways and nearly choked by a hand on his collar. Boris' black eyes glared at him. He flapped his great oily wings and they soared upwards. Vlad was dragged through his bedroom window and dropped on the floor.

Vlad scrabbled back against the wall and pulled himself upright, panting for breath.

Gretchen laughed. "What an idiot you are, Vlad. You know you can't fly. Oh, I've had a brilliant idea. Boris, let's play catch."

"For once you've come up with something worth listening to. It's such good fun when the prey screams," Boris said.

The twins made a grab for Vlad and dragged him to the window. He fought against them, until Boris smacked his head against the wall.

Blood dripped into his eyes. He doubled over, desperate to drag air into his lungs, but he couldn't breathe out to let the new air in. He looked up, wiping away the blood to clear his vision, and saw Gretchen's coal-black eyes gleaming as she laughed.

She danced around the room. "The freak can't fly, he's going to die. Eee-oh-eye, the freak's gonna die."

Her voice was like warm honey and chocolate, sweet, smooth and beautiful, but Vlad hated it.

"I love this game," she said. "Boris, shout when you drop him. I'll count to three before I fly down to catch poor, poor little Vlad."

"If he falls all the way down there's no fun in it for us," Boris said.

"I know that, stupid. So you make sure you fly really high before you let him go." She smiled at Vlad. "If you were a proper vampire, you'd be able to fly, too, but you're not, are you? You're just a stupid hupyre."

Vlad tried to answer, but couldn't.

"Urhhh, urhhhh, urhhh," Gretchen mocked. "Go on then, Boris. Take him."

Boris turned into bat form. Vlad tried to run, but Gretchen blocked the doorway. He fought and kicked as he was lifted and dragged out of the bedroom window. He clung to his cousin as they flew upwards, higher and higher. If Boris let him go now, he'd surely die. His stomach flipped and he nearly threw up.

The castle was a tiny speck far below. Boris let go and Vlad dropped like lead, gathering speed as he plunged. Faster and faster he plummeted. The night wind pulled at his face as the castle raced towards him.

* * *

Mary and Joe Greening heard Vlad scream. They looked up into the bright moonlit sky to see his tiny figure dropping.

"Oh, lordy, lordy, it's master Vlad," gasped Mary. She punched Joe's shoulder. "Do something, do something! Don't stand there like an oaf. Save my poor lambkins."

"How on earth do you expect me to save a child who's hurtling through the air?"

"Think, Joe, think!" Mary ordered, thumping him again.

"What about the baskets I use for gathering peaches? We could pack them with straw."

"We haven't enough time, Joe."

Then the screaming stopped. Gretchen had flown out of the castle window and caught Vlad. She soared upwards, dragging Vlad with her. Up and up she went, far past the point at which Boris had dropped him. Mary and Joe watched as Gretchen turned in an elegant arc and then let go. Once again Vlad's screaming tore through the night as he plummeted.

"Quick, Mary, throw some straw in this basket. Maybe we can catch him. It might work if they drop him over us."

"But what about if they take him over there and let him fall on the rocks?"

"We'd better just hope they don't, Mary. We can't help him then."

She and Joe picked up the stuffed basket and ran to and fro.

"Mind my tomatoes," yelled Joe. "They's about ready for picking."

They careered back and forth, destroying the better part of the year's work Joe had put in. The screaming stopped. This time Boris caught Vlad and carried him back up into the night.

"Oh, I can't bear it, Joe. My poor little master."

* * *

Vlad clung to Boris' legs, determined not to be dropped again, but it didn't help. His cousin lunged and bit into Vlad's fingers. He let go and fell from an even higher point than before. The air rushed past, catching at his jacket. His arms flapped as fast as a windmill in a storm and, suddenly, he stopped in midair. He wagged his arms furiously. His legs felt like they were being crunched as they got shorter. His arms pulled away from his body and spread, until his jacket turned into silky wings. Vlad flapped them and for the first time in his life he flew. He stretched his new wings and soared. I'm doing it, he thought, I'm actually doing it. I'm flying! I'm a superhero, a flying machine, Wonder Bat …

The soaring sensation disappeared. His legs stretched out again, his wings changed back into his jacket and he plummeted. He flapped his arms, whirled them as before. No good. He felt the mouthful of peach he'd eaten leave his stomach and clog his throat. He swallowed and screamed at Joe and Mary far below.

"Catch meeeeeeeeeeeeeee …"

Tears flew from his eyes as his stomach did somersaults.

"Pleeeeeeeeeeeeeeeease ..." he screamed.

He saw Boris swooping in from the left and flapped harder, but it only turned him in the opposite direction. Gretchen was coming at him from the right. He was trapped. He closed his eyes and tried to remember the bat sensations, but still he dropped.

Boris was only yards away, and closing fast, but Gretchen was faster. Vlad was just feet above the lawn in front of the castle. He flapped his arms harder, harder, faster, faster. Then with a whoomph, he felt the crunch and pull of his limbs changing. His vision shrank to a pinprick. He became a bat once more and shot straight up; only just avoiding Gretchen's outstretched claws on one side and Boris' on the other. Behind him he heard his cousins collide with a sickening crunch.

He didn't stop to see if they were hurt, but swooped over to Mary and Joe's cottage.

"Look at meeeeeeeeeeeeeeeee," he screamed, delighted at their shocked faces.

He flew towards freedom – the fields on the far side of Dank Forest.

Never had anything felt so good. He loved

the feel of the air rushing past. He flapped his wings with all his might and wondered if he dared try to loop-the-loop. He was invincible. Saviour of Magdorovia.

After a few minutes his body changed again. He tried to control his bat shape. If he fell now he'd land in the forest. He flapped his wings, but no longer had control. They were changing back to his jacket. He dropped, crashing into the roof of a tree. Tumbling down through the branches, sharp twigs scratched his face and hands. Crash, thump, crash, he bounced on every branch before landing with a thud, forcing all the air from his lungs.

He lay still, too scared to move. Then, wheezing, he heaved himself to a sitting position and grabbed his inhaler from his pocket. When his breath returned at last, he stood up. Apart from the blood running down his face and a twinge in one ankle, he was okay. He checked, no bones broken. Great. But the blood on his face worried him. Werewolves would smell it. He grabbed some leaves and rubbed.

"Ow," he yelled as the leaves stung the cuts and grazes. Then he looked around in case he'd been heard by someone. Or something.

He edged backwards into the safety of a tree trunk behind him. It was dark in the forest, but at least the moon was full and he could see. It could have been worse. The thought of being in the forest in total darkness made him shudder. He thought about the werewolves. The full moon brought them out. Then he realised he was grinning, even though he was scared. He'd flown, *and* escaped from the family's clutches. Huh, he wasn't so useless, after all. Okay, he might not be Super Bat, but he was still pretty nifty.

Thoughts of where to go next made all his good feelings disappear. He came away from the tree into a small clearing and turned round and round. He had to decide which way to go. No, first he had to decide *where* to go. Mary and Joe would help him find his parents, but their cottage was so close to the castle. No matter how hard he tried, he couldn't think of anyone else. He had no food and no money. That reminded him how hungry he was. A tear stung his eye, but he brushed it away. There was no point in crying. He might just as well yell to the werewolves to come and get him. Okay, Mary and Joe's it would have to be, but which way was that?

He peered through the gloom. In every direction, massive trees and fallen branches blocked his path.

A lone cloud sailed across the moon and the forest turned black. His breath shortened and he started to gasp. *Stop it. The werewolves will hear.* The cloud passed over and the clearing lit up again. He saw a moving shadow and froze. The shadow grew, came closer and closer. A rank animal stench drifted on the night air as the shadow approached the clearing. Twigs snapped and leaves rustled as it got nearer. Then, just as Vlad was about to turn and run, the creature broke through the trees. An enormous deer stopped, peered at Vlad, and then trotted away.

Tears of relief made muddy tracks down Vlad's cheeks. He was lost in the forest, his family wanted to kill him, his only friends lived near the castle and life just ... wasn't ... fair!

He fell to his knees and sobbed until his tears were all used up. Sniffing, he found his lost courage. He couldn't stay in the forest forever.

He had to decide which direction to take. No problem, he'd fly above the trees and see where he was. He listened. No sound of anything moving. He edged his way to the middle of the clearing and tried to think bat thoughts. He imagined floating on the wind, screwed his eyes up, and pictured the forest through tiny bat vision. Then with his eyes half-closed, he peered around to make sure nothing was about to leap on him and flapped his arms. Nothing happened. He flapped them harder, then harder still. Nothing. Not even a twinge in his bones.

Okay, he'd flown like a bat, so maybe some of the other vampire skills would work. Everyone knew bats had built-in sonar; he'd use his to decide which way to go. He concentrated hard and felt echo waves leave his body, bounce off a building some distance away and come back. The force of the returning waves nearly knocked him off his feet. *Wow, oh wow, oh wow.* It was the first time he'd used sonar and his success cheered him up. He tested his ankle. It was a bit sore, but not too bad. He'd be able to walk on it. He set off in the direction the sonic waves felt strongest, but a huge pile of fallen branches blocked the way, so he scrambled over them. As he hit the ground on the other side he heard trees rustling. Was it the deer coming back again?

No, the animal smell was different. It was like sweaty feet mixed with mouldy cheese. He'd never seen one, but he knew, deep inside he knew, werewolves were coming.

Chapter Three

Everything's at Stake

Valentyna and Viktor arrived at Vlad's bedroom with Timms, only to find the room empty. The delightful sound of a child screaming in fear drew Valentyna to the window.

"Oh listen! Viktor, they're playing catch."

"Tell them not to drop him. We need Vlad to decipher the verse," he reminded her.

She leant out and called, but couldn't see the twins.

"They must be round the front of the castle. Come on, let's go and find them."

The two vampires herded the terrified lawyer along the corridor, down the marble stairs, into the great hall, out through the gigantic oak door, across the courtyard and over the moat. Valentyna screamed at her children to bring

Vlad back, but they either didn't hear or didn't want to hear, because the game continued.

"Viktor, you'd better go and …" she began, stopping short at the sight of Vlad actually flying.

She howled with rage as Gretchen's head connected with Boris' ribs and their wings returned to clothing. In a flurry of limbs, wings and clothes they dropped, only regaining their bat shapes inches from the ground.

"You bleedin' idiots," Valentyna screeched. "You've let 'im go 'an we need 'im for the lawyer."

She stopped as her words reached her ears and she realised she'd gone all common.

"Ahem, what I meant to say was, you foolish children. You've allowed him to escape and we need him because the lawyer is here. Viktor, go after him."

"No need, my love. Look!" Viktor said, drawing her into his arms.

She followed the line of his pointing finger and saw Vlad fall from the sky. "Good. At least we know where to find him. Timms, you wait here for us. Timms …" There was no sign of the lawyer. "Where did he go? He was here just now."

She looked around and saw a speck disappearing into the forest at the end of the long driveway.

"Now what are we supposed to do? Get him back, Viktor. Now!" she commanded, careful this time not to lose her posh accent.

"I think we should go and find my nephew first, dearest," Viktor said. "We can call for the lawyer once we have Vlad safely in our clutches again. Just think how much pleasure we'll have dropping Vlad back in the forest once he's explained the rhyme to us," he said with a smile.

Her heart melted. When Viktor smiled, death was sure to follow. What a man.

"Let's go now, this second," she said.

"But of course, my dear one. Children," Viktor shouted, "stop trying to kill each other. Come, we're going hupyre hunting."

Flying in Black Arrow formation, children inside, parents outside, they took to the air and searched the forest for signs of movement. They'd been flying for nearly half an hour when Boris yelled.

"There! I saw some branches moving down there on the left."

The vampires hovered, peering at the thick, dark mass of foliage.

"Where?" asked Gretchen. "You've made it up."

"Branches moved. They did," Boris snarled. "It's about time you started giving me some respect. I'm the oldest and don't you forget it."

"By two minutes," Gretchen jeered.

"Never mind," said Viktor. "We'll fly on until …"

"There! Look there!" Boris' gleeful voice cut across his father's words.

They looked in the direction of Boris' pointing wing and, sure enough, the branches moved as though someone was pushing through the trees.

"Yes!" screamed Valentyna. "Let's go."

Vlad, once again within their grasp, wouldn't escape this time. They swooped down and landed in the area where the trees had been moving.

As they settled back into human form, the foul odour of sweaty feet assailed their sensitive nostrils. A wall of staring yellow eyes surrounded the vampires. As a pack, the werewolves closed in, teeth bared.

"Up, up, up," Viktor bellowed.

Resuming bat shape, they took off with less grace than usual, only just avoiding the snapping jaws of the leaping werewolves.

Scrambling skywards, they forced their way through the dense overhanging branches. They didn't bother with pretty formation patterns. It was safety first and elegance last in their rush to get back to the castle.

The four dark shapes swooped through the open window and landed in a dishevelled heap on the library floor. Valentyna resumed her human form, shaking her long, black hair free of twigs and leaves. Viktor changed next, and looked with disgust at his ripped clothing. The twins changed shape and immediately began to attack each other. For once, Valentyna wasn't proud of their vicious streak.

"I've 'ad enough," she screeched. "Gerrout!" She stopped and took a deep breath. That was twice in one night she'd gone common. That puny hupyre was going to suffer for making her lose her social skills. "Go and play elsewhere," she said in perfectly cultured tones, "but first change your clothes. Vampires are well-dressed at all times. *Especially* upper-class vampires like us. You two look like scarecrows."

Boris stopped thumping Gretchen, who'd been trying to break his arm, and they sidled towards the door.

"Yes, Mama," Boris whined, "but Gretchen started it."

Gretchen opened her mouth, but no sound came out. Valentyna lifted herself off the ground and hovered over them. With her hair flying in several different directions, eyes like hot coals and fangs bared, she no longer looked anything like the mother they could twist around their batwings. She'd turned into a vision from their worst daymare. They fled.

As the sound of the twins' racing footsteps faded, Valentyna floated to the ground. She had to control her temper.

"I ... want ... to ... kill ... him," she said, forcing herself to take a deep breath between each word.

"My precious love, my deep delight, my little demon of the dark," cooed Viktor. "Calm yourself. We know he fell into the forest. If the werewolves were prepared to attack the four of us, just imagine what they'll do to a weedy little hupyre like Vlad."

"That's all well and good, Viktor, but once he's dead so is our chance of finding out the rhyme."

"No, my precious one, with Vlad chewed up, the situation is better than it was before. I'll send for Timms. As the heir to Castle Malign, the lawyer will have no choice but to tell me the verse. Between us, I'm sure we can decode it and work out where the treasure is kept."

She melted as he took her hand and kissed each fingertip.

* * *

Vlad grabbed an overhead branch and dragged himself up. He'd never climbed a tree so quickly, but fear drove him on. He found a safe perch at the top and peered down through the leaves.

About twenty wolf shapes loped around the base of the tree, sniffing the air and howling. Vlad knew they could smell him. He could barely breathe. Never had it been so hard to get air into his lungs. He felt sick and started to shake. Grabbing a branch, he clung to his high refuge.

He heard the howls of another pack in the distance. The forest must be full of werewolves. His hunters paced below him, showing no sign of giving up. He wondered if he should attempt to fly, but if he fell here he would be eaten for sure. Not even his vampire side could survive being chewed to bits.

Suddenly, the werewolves stopped circling his tree. Ears all pricked in one direction, they listened and then turned. Vlad peered through the gloom to see what had caught their attention. The deer that had startled him earlier was coming towards the pack.

Vlad had to do something, but what? Reaching out, he pulled several acorns from a nearby branch. Maybe he could distract the werewolves. He inched his way to his feet and clung to the branch with one arm. He threw the acorns as hard as he could in the opposite direction to the deer. Thank goodness for the full moon. The nuts rustled through the trees and the werewolves turned and loped towards the sound. Vlad was relieved to see the deer stop and scamper back the way it had come.

The werewolves must have realised they'd been tricked because they soon returned and bounded after the retreating deer. Vlad could only hope that the poor animal got away. When the werewolves were out of sight, he came down from his perch and crept away; terrified they might hear him and come back, he held his breath for as long as he could.

Every few yards he stopped to listen to the night sounds and sniff the air. Owls hooted and screeched, but at least he couldn't smell any werewolves. Tired, he rested against a tree. The leaves rustled as if someone was shaking them and he turned, the sick feeling in his stomach rushing up towards his mouth. A hawk flew out from the top of the tree and he gasped with relief. He'd never realised before how sinister leaves could sound. He trudged on, as fast as he could, constantly looking over his shoulder. It felt as though *something* was watching his every move.

He used his newfound sonic pinging skill every few yards. The force of the echo returned stronger each time, so he must be going in the right direction. He hadn't realised he'd flown so far over the forest before falling and kept looking up, hoping to see the turrets of his castle appearing above the treetops.

He stopped. There it was again. A faint sound on the very edge of his hearing. He looked all around. Did he just see a branch move? Someone was out there, he was sure of it. He strained to see. But, no matter how hard he scanned the trees, there was nothing there.

He'd never felt so alone. The forest whispered with the sounds of nocturnal creatures. Every time an owl hooted, Vlad's heart stopped.

It felt as if he'd walked and crawled for miles before he glimpsed a light through the trees and ran towards it. As he got to the edge of the forest, gasping for breath, he realised his sonic ability was about as bad as his flying skills. He hadn't walked towards the castle and the safety of Mary's cottage at all. He'd gone in the opposite direction and arrived at Malign village.

The light he'd seen came from a lantern hanging above the doorway of the village pub. The glow illuminated a creaking sign. The picture of a vampire with a piece of wood through his heart and the words Ye Olde Stake House left Vlad in no doubt of the landlord's feelings. A blackboard rested against the wall with the house specialities written in chalk.

Steak 'n' chips – 2 rupeks

Steak 'n' mash – 2 rupeks

Steak 'n' baked potato – 2 rupeks

Stake in vampire – no charge

He turned and peered into the darkness behind him. Which was safer, to go on or to go back? A twig cracked. Leaves rustled. He stepped into the clearing and away from the forest.

An old man sat on a bench outside the pub,

head slumped forward in sleep. Vlad decided he looked kindly and crept towards him. When he was halfway between the forest and the pub, a door banged inside the building. The old man opened one eye, gave a sudden start and jumped up.

"Vampires," he shouted. "Quick, quick. They's attacking us. Quick, vampires."

The doors burst open and several burly men surged into the street. Vlad froze in mid-stride as they glared at him.

"Cedric, you old fool, that's no vampire."

"'tis, 'tis. I'd know one anywhere. I remember …"

"Don't start your remembering again or we'll be out here all night. Look at his hair, it's the wrong colour."

"Doesn't matter – he's got the teeth. Shove some garlic in his mouth."

"I'm not taking a chance on getting that close. There's a bowl of holy water inside. I'll go and fetch a glassful to chuck over him."

"Garlic's best. I remember …"

Vlad turned and ran back to the forest. He pushed aside branches, climbed over huge tree roots and scrambled through bushes. Behind him the sounds of pursuit gradually faded. He hobbled as fast as his painful ankle allowed, deeper and deeper into the heart of Dank Forest.

Finally, he stopped to catch his breath. A branch broke and he got up to run, but was thrown to the ground before he'd gone a few steps. Pinned down by large hairy paws, he looked up into two fierce orbs.

Pools of yellow fire glared down at him. The eyes were surrounded by tufts of hair. Each tuft, completely separate from the next, was a different length and shade of brown. The wide mouth looked full of the wickedest teeth Vlad had ever seen so close to his face. Even his vampire cousins hadn't looked as menacing. The sweaty feet smell of werewolf breath was even worse close up. Vlad trembled and felt the old familiar tightening of his chest. He wheezed and one of the paws clamped over his mouth. He couldn't speak, couldn't breathe. His eyes pleaded with the creature to let him go. The shaggy head moved from side to side.

Vlad heard leaves rustling. The noises were getting closer. Again the creature shook his head.

A pack of werewolves ran through the trees nearby. He could feel the fear coming from his captor. Was the creature helping him, or making sure he didn't have to share his prize?

Eventually the sound of the pack grew fainter and Vlad felt the pressure on his mouth lessen. The werewolf let go, stood up and bared his teeth. Vlad backed away. The werewolf followed and reached out his paws, grimacing.

Vlad turned and ran. The werewolf was close behind him and gaining all the time. Vlad couldn't breathe, but fear drove him on. Just when he thought he might get away, he was thrown to the ground. Once again the werewolf's paw closed over Vlad's mouth, sweat dripping from its hideous face.

Vlad heard voices and strained to free himself, but the werewolf's grip tightened. If only he could get the creature's paw away from his mouth he could scream for help.

The voices grew closer. Vlad peered through the trees in the direction of the sound. He saw two men in a clearing. One was tall, with a craggy face topped by a greasy-looking fur hat. His trousers and jacket seemed to be made of the same fur. Across his chest he wore two ammunition belts. Silver bullets glinted in the moonlight. He had a long rifle slung over one shoulder and a dead werewolf over the other.

His partner was about a foot shorter, dressed in black and had a patch over one eye. He didn't have a rifle, but he had two ammunition belts across his chest. Garlic cloves and crucifixes dangled from one. On the other belt tiny bottles made tinkling noises when he moved. Across his back he had a quiver with half a dozen sharpened sticks and swinging from his belt was a mallet.

The tall man peered all around. "I can smell 'em, I'm telling yer. Near here, not too far. I can smell werewolf."

"Yeah, yeah, Skinner. You always can. You should sell that nose of yourn, it's worth a fortune. It can smell invisible werewolves."

Skinner hawked and spat. "Well at least I've made a kill tonight, which is more than you have." He patted the dead werewolf. "A nice fee I'll get for this beauty, Bones. Where's yours, hey?"

"I'll get some bats, don't you worry about that. No vampire gets past me. I've heard there's a nest not far from here."

The werewolf hunter laughed. "You don't fancy a trip up to Castle Malign? I've heard there's new vampires up there now. Scarier than the last lot."

Bones scowled and adjusted his ammunition belt. "I'm not going there tonight, no. But they're on my list. I ain't scared of no vampire. What's more, I ain't leaving this forest until I've killed one."

Bounty hunters! Vlad was trapped between a werewolf and a vampire bounty hunter. His chest closed and he could feel the urge to gulp in air. He tried to control it. Don't make a noise, he told himself. Don't make a ... Don't make ...

His stomach rumbled, sending loud, gurgling hunger signals into the night.

Chapter Four

Hunger Pangs

Timms' front door vibrated to a furious hammering and he hurried to put a stop to the racket.

Bang-a-bang-*bang*.Bang-a-bang-*bang*.Bang-a-bang-*bang*.

"Okay, okay! I'm coming. Sssh! You'll disturb Mrs Timms."

He opened the door and got punched on the nose. Through watering eyes he glared at his assailant.

"Why'd you hit me?"

"I'm so sorry, sir," the man said. "I didn't mean to. You put your nose where the knocker was."

Timms was about to shout at him when he realised it was a servant from Castle Malign.

His stomach flipped at the sight of the scarlet uniform's gold fang-shaped buttons glinting in the torchlight.

"Communication for you, sir. They want you up at the castle as soon as possible. Acting Count Viktor says to tell you not to hang around, but to get a move on."

"They want me now? Again? Please don't say I have to go again."

"Sorry, sir. I just deliver the messages. What's the grub like at Ye Olde Stake House?"

"What?"

"Ye Olde Stake House. I thought I'd see if the place was still open for a quick bite before reporting back to the castle."

The words 'a quick bite' made him shiver. Timms shut his eyes and grabbed his stomach, which felt full of wriggling worms.

When he opened his eyes again, the messenger had disappeared. He closed the door. Back to the castle? He'd barely escaped on the last visit. With a bit of luck, Mrs Timms would forbid him to go.

He returned to the sitting room. Mrs Timms' sat upright on a hard-backed chair, knitting needles flashing as yet another scarf took shape.

"I've been ordered up to the castle, dearest," he said.

"You're quivering. You know how I dislike it when you quiver."

"Mrs Timms, my dear," he said and coughed nervously.

"Get on with it," she commanded, her knitting needles moving so fast that sparks flew.

"Mrs, er …" he paused and gulped at her glaring face. "The new owners, well not exactly owners, but if they get rid of the child, that is, if he … if … they're not nice people," he finished in a rush.

Mrs Timms' face turned a funny purple colour. Her knitting needles blurred and started to smoke.

"Not nice people? *Not nice people*? They don't have to be nice to pay the bills. You get up to that castle right now. They wouldn't have sent for you if it wasn't important."

He sighed and went to get some vampire protection. Half an hour later, having checked for the umpteenth time that he had garlic in every pocket, he set out in the pony and trap for the castle. His neck drooped with the weight of the enormous cross hidden under his shirt and he'd drenched his clothes with extra holy water, but still he didn't feel safe.

* * *

Vlad clutched at his stomach in a vain attempt to stop the gurgling. The noise seemed to get louder and louder. Then it stopped, just as suddenly as it had started.

Skinner yelled. "Bones, Bones, come back. Did you hear that?"

"Hear what?" Bones shouted from far off. "You adding super hearing to that super smelling talent of yourn? I'm off to hunt some vamps. You coming with me, or hanging around here all night?"

Go with him, Vlad thought. Please, please go with him.

"I thought I heard something, not sure what. Yeah, okay, I might as well go your way. Where are you heading?"

Vlad and the creature holding him stayed as still as statues until the rustling of branches disappeared completely. Great, at least one threat had gone. All he had to worry about now was being eaten by a werewolf.

The grip on his mouth relaxed, but the creature still held him fast around the waist.

"Don't run. I won't hurt you," it whispered. "If I let you go, do you promise not to shout and bring those men back?"

Vlad nodded. The creature released his grip and turned.

Enormous jagged teeth held Vlad enthralled. He couldn't tear his eyes away.

Vlad's feet itched to run, but how far would he get? Then he realised the werewolf was attempting to smile. Not that Vlad felt much safer, as it showed even more teeth, but he did relax a little. The thing had saved him from the bounty hunters. The creature wasn't like the other werewolves he'd seen. This one was neither wolf nor human.

He was a higgledy-piggledy mixture of the two. His arms were covered in hair and ended in paws, but he was wearing trousers on what looked like, as far as Vlad could tell, human legs. He had a canvass bag slung over one shoulder. Most of his face was free from hair apart from the peculiar tufts around his enormous yellow eyes. His lips looked human, but those teeth sure were terrifying. Vlad prayed he could trust him and smiled back, showing his own sharp incisors.

"Wha … what do you want?" he asked, forcing himself not to scream.

"I don't want anything. Tell me, are you what I think you are? Are you a hupyre? Keep your voice down in case those two come back," it hissed and then contorted its face into the worst grimace Vlad had yet seen.

"Yes, I'm a hupyre," he whispered.

"Oh yesssssss," the werewolf hissed.

Vlad didn't like the way the werewolf was staring at him, but then it held out a paw.

"I'm Rexus," he said. "Sorry, I didn't think hupyres really existed. I've always wanted to meet one."

The werewolf stood with his paw extended and Vlad felt obliged to shake it.

"I'm Vlad Malign. How did you know about those men?" Vlad whispered.

"Twice now Skinner's had me in his sights with his rifle. If one of his silver bullets hit me, I'd be done for."

Vlad shuddered. "The other one, the one Skinner called Bones, he's after vampires, but he'd kill me, too, wouldn't he?"

"Yes, but let's not worry about them right now. What are you doing in the forest?"

Vlad sighed. "It's a long story. I've escaped

from my aunt and uncle up at Castle Malign, but I need to go back there. Which way is it?"

Vlad's stomach rumbled so loudly that Rexus jumped.

"You'll have the hunters back here in no time if you make noises like that," the werewolf hissed.

"I can't help it, I'm starving," Vlad whispered back. "Do you know the way to the castle?"

"What do you want to go back there for if you've only just escaped? Come to that, why did you need to escape?"

"It's a long story. I don't want to go to the actual castle, but I need to get to some friends who live nearby. I don't have any money or food and I need somewhere to stay while I figure out what to do next."

"My granny's cottage isn't too far from here. She'll give you something to eat. You could stay with us for tonight. Granny makes a great casserole."

"Um, a casserole sounds nice," Vlad said. "But I don't eat meat. I'm a vegetarian," he finished in a rush, determined to get the truth out straight away.

"I don't care what you are, as long as you're a hupyre. And to think I didn't believe they existed," Rexus said. "Come with me. Granny will be *so* pleased to see you."

Vlad didn't like the werewolf's hungry look. But if he was going to eat him, surely he'd have attacked by now. The werewolf took a step towards him and Vlad steeled himself not to run.

"We're alike you and me," Rexus said putting an arm round Vlad's shoulders. "I'm no longer a proper werewolf and I'm not yet human either. The werewolves hate me and, when I look like this, the humans want to kill me. I know just how you feel, Vlad. Neither one species, nor the other."

"Um, what do you mean? Haven't you always looked like you do now?"

"No," Rexus said. "I used to be a full werewolf. Granny says with a bit of luck and a waning moon, I could be human all the time."

"What?" said Vlad. "I didn't understand that last bit."

"It's just my little joke," Rexus said. "Come on, you'll be safer in Granny's cottage than roaming the forest on your own."

Vlad hesitated.

"What's wrong? You think I'm going to eat you? Let's see how long you last on your own," Rexus snarled and strode off.

Vlad ran after him. "Don't leave me. I'm sorry. It's just that it feels like everyone I meet wants me dead."

Rexus gave a strange toothy smile.

"Not me. I *definitely* don't want you dead. Come on; let's go to Granny's. You'll feel better once you've had something to eat."

Vlad followed Rexus through the forest towards Hungerton, a village about three miles from Malign. Rexus was right about one thing, before he tried to get back to Mary and Joe's he needed food and rest.

They pushed on through some bushes and came up against the hard black eyes of Skinner staring down the sights of his rifle.

"I knew I could smell werewolf," he said. "Your stench is like perfume to me and my nose never lies."

He cocked the rifle and settled the stock back into his shoulder.

"Don't you want to try running? I much prefer a moving target. It's more sporting."

Vlad could smell fear coming from Rexus. The werewolf was trembling. Vlad glared at the man holding the rifle – he was enjoying Rexus' fear. Anger such as he'd never known before surged through him. This evil man was going to kill Rexus.

Vlad felt his eyes changing. His vision reduced to tiny pinpricks of light, completely focussed on the man with the gun. Skinner caressed the trigger ready to fire.

"Noooooooo," Vlad screamed.

He lifted off the ground and flew at Skinner, burning with rage. Drain him, his brain screamed; drain him of every drop. Bite deep into the jugular. Blood! Suck him dry …

Skinner squealed and sprinted away through the trees. Vlad dropped to his knees, wheezing. What on earth had happened to him? He shook with fear. He was scared. Really scared. He could still feel the urge, the desire, blood, he needed … Rexus stood in front of him. Vlad stared at the werewolf's neck.

"You saved my life," Rexus said. "I shouldn't think Skinner will stop running until he gets to the other side of the forest. Damn it, this makes it harder for me …"

Vlad tried to speak, but he couldn't get any words out. He shook himself. Think of peaches. Peaches, peaches, *peaches – not, blood*. Finally, with thoughts of sweet peach juice, he brought his urge to bite Rexus under control and stood up.

"Is your granny's cottage far from here? I, er, I really am *very* hungry."

Half an hour later they came to a clearing in the forest. In the middle was a cottage, even smaller than Mary and Joe's. Neat garden beds lined the path leading to the front door and the sweet smell of herbs perfumed the air. Rexus led the way to the front door and pushed down the door handle.

"Come on in. Don't stand outside."

Vlad stepped into an entrance hall. Stairs on the right leading to the upper floor almost filled the space, barely leaving enough room to walk through to the rest of the cottage. Vlad had never been inside anywhere so tiny and wondered how two people could live there. It hardly seemed big enough for one, never mind a granny and a werewolf.

"Granny, we've got a visitor. A *hupyre*. Vlad from the castle needs somewhere to stay tonight," Rexus called out.

Vlad's stomach rumbled.

"Oh, and he needs feeding," Rexus added.

A sweet-faced old woman with white curls peeping out from under a night bonnet appeared from a door at the back of the hall.

She had a floral shawl draped around her shoulders. It seemed in danger of falling to the ground with every step she took.

"A hupyre? Really? What did you say your name was? Vlad? What a wonderful night, I mean name," she said.

Feeling shy, Vlad hung back. The woman came towards him, untangling the trailing shawl which appeared to have a life of its own.

"I'm Granny Entwhistle. Come into the sitting room, child, and you can tell me how you came to meet up with Rexus."

The room was even smaller than Vlad had thought it could be. Two sofas faced each other, but, as tiny as they were, they almost filled the room. He edged his way around one and stood between them.

"I'm sorry to intrude, Mrs Entwhistle," he began.

"Oh, you must call me Granny."

Vlad smiled. "Er, Granny, I'm sorry to intrude."

The smell of a casserole wafted from the kitchen. His mouth watered and his stomach groaned.

"Please, I'm so hungry. Could I have something to eat?"

"Of course, you poor child. Come through to the kitchen."

"He doesn't eat meat, Granny. I'll have his share."

"No need, Rexus," she said and winked. "I made a vegetable casserole tonight. Well now, isn't that fortunate?"

The kitchen was almost the same size as the sitting room. One wall was entirely taken up with a black cooking range. Above it hung a rack with pots, cooking utensils and several bunches of herbs hanging from it. On the range a black pot bubbled and the aroma of freshly cooked vegetables made Vlad tremble. It was days since he'd last eaten proper food.

Rexus took the canvass bag from his shoulder and dumped it on the table. Vlad thought he saw it move. He stared for a while, but it stayed still. His imagination was working overtime. Funny what hunger can do, he thought.

Granny Entwhistle ladled out casserole. When his bowl was placed in front of him he had to stop himself from grabbing the spoon and shovelling food into his mouth.

"Eat up, Vlad," she said. "Don't be shy."

He needed no second telling. He'd once read about nectar, the food of the gods, but he knew it couldn't possibly taste as good as this casserole.

In no time at all he was wiping the inside of the bowl with bread to clean up every last scrap. He put down his spoon and explained to Granny how he'd escaped and met up with Rexus.

"And *he saved my life*, Granny. Old Skinner nearly got me," Rexus said, patting a paw on Vlad's back.

Vlad squirmed, remembering how much he'd wanted to suck the bounty hunter dry. Even worse, how tasty Rexus had looked once Skinner had run off. He'd never felt like that before and never wanted to again.

Granny put another bowlful in front of each of them and Vlad picked up the spoon. Rexus stuck his nose into his bowl and slurped. Vlad tried not to stare when Rexus looked up and used his long pointy tongue to hook a piece of onion hanging from the end of his nose. He'd been so intent on eating the first helping he hadn't even noticed Rexus couldn't use a spoon.

"Get stuck in, Vlad. You'll feel much better with a full stomach. When we've finished you and Rexus can help me move the donkeys into the barn for the night."

After Vlad had finished the second bowl, leaving him feeling as though his stomach was bigger than the cottage, they all went out to see to George and Gladys.

"You can help me take care of them while you're here. They're a bit stubborn, but it's their age," said Granny as her shawl slithered to the ground.

"I'd love to help, but I'll be leaving in the morning."

Vlad picked up the wispy-looking material, surprised at how warm and heavy it was. As he handed it to Granny, it felt almost alive.

"Nonsense," she said as the shawl settled into place around her shoulders. "You must stay with us for a few days."

He smiled, not sure how to say he wanted to leave without appearing ungrateful. He scratched George's head.

"How old is George?"

"He's fifteen and Gladys is twelve and one," said Granny.

"And one what?"

"Not *what* anything, just twelve and one. We don't use the proper word for the number between twelve and fourteen in my house. It brings too much bad luck if it's said out loud."

Vlad realised he had a lot to learn about the outside world.

They went back to the kitchen. He'd only ever lived in Castle Malign and had never been in a place as small as this. He felt awkward and saw himself as an intruder in Granny's home.

"Don't stand there, Vlad. Come and sit down," Granny said. "You *must* rest with us for at least a few days. I'd be happy for you to stay longer, but we already have problems with the villagers from Hungerton. People are scared of anything that's different. That's why I moved out here just after my poor daughter died giving birth to Rexus. When I realised he was a werewolf, I knew the villagers would turn on him. Only folk who need help from me come this far into the forest," she said with a sigh.

"I thought I'd go back to the castle tomorrow and stay with Mary and Joe," said Vlad.

"No!" shouted Rexus and Granny together.

Granny frowned at Rexus. "I don't think that's a good idea at all," she said. "Your aunt and uncle will know your friends would help you, so they'll be watching their cottage, that's for sure. Don't you have any family on your mother's side?"

"Only my aunt Elsabetta," Vlad said without much hope. "She lives in Malign village. I've never met her. She didn't like it when my mum and dad got married, I don't know why. Maybe she didn't like my dad. Um, did you know my father?" he asked.

"I only knew of him, I'd never met him. Why?"

"Because I don't believe he killed anybody, but my aunt and uncle said the villagers attacked my parents when they were out walking one evening. They said my father had taken a village child … and … and. …"

"Your father didn't take that child," Granny said.

She looked across at Rexus on the opposite sofa.

"Tell Vlad what you saw."

"The man looked like your father," Rexus began, "but it wasn't him. I was in the forest when I heard a scream. I ran as fast as I could, and got there just before the vampire changed into a bat and flew away. The villagers from Malign arrived soon after I did. They were sure it was your dad, but it wasn't."

He put a paw on Vlad's arm.

"I've seen the Count many times and I know

it wasn't him. I was in human form at the time and told the mob that it wasn't Count Ilya, but no one wanted to listen."

"I miss my mum and dad so much. Sometimes I think they must be dead or surely they'd come back for me. But inside, deep inside, I'm certain they're alive and in trouble."

Granny put her arm around Vlad's shoulders.

"Don't worry. We're here for you. I think Rexus should pay a visit to your aunt Elsabetta tomorrow morning."

"I'll go with him. I can go out in daylight as long as it isn't too sunny."

Granny shook her head. "I don't think it's a good idea for you to be seen in Malign village. Rexus should go on his own. By day no one will take any notice of him, but you look too much like a vampire, even with your fair hair, and the villagers might turn on you," Granny said.

"Okay," said Vlad, "but I'll go with him to the edge of the village. I just hope my aunt won't turn me away because she's still mad at my parents."

As he finished speaking, the bag on the table heaved as though something inside was looking for a way out.

"It's moving," he said, pointing as the bag shifted across the table.

Granny snatched it up. "Oh, that's just some herbs. Rexus gathers them for me during the full moon."

"But there's something else in there. It moved," Vlad said.

Granny opened the bag and showed Vlad the contents. There was nothing apart from a mixture of greenery. But, as he turned away, he thought he caught a glimpse of some tiny eyes looking up at him. He looked again, but the eyes had vanished.

"I thought I saw a mouse, but, but …"

"You're overtired. Let's get you up to bed," said Granny. "You can sleep in Rexus' room for tonight and he'll sleep on the sofa in the sitting room."

Vlad followed her up a narrow staircase and into the tiniest bedroom he'd ever seen. It had a single bed pushed against one wall and a chest of drawers and washstand against the opposite wall, with just enough room for him to squeeze between them.

He lit a candle, then turned back to thank Granny. With the lantern light on the landing shining behind her she looked different. It was like an optical illusion he'd once seen where two women were in the same drawing. Vlad could see a second Granny just on the edge of his vision, but when he tried to bring it forward, that image disappeared.

Granny reached towards him and patted his arm.

"Goodnight, Vlad. You get a good night's sleep and you'll feel better tomorrow."

He shut the door as she left, feeling safer once he'd turned the key.

* * *

Rexus looked up as Granny came back into the sitting room. Gone was the sweet little old lady. In her place strode a woman with bright red hair and green eyes so vivid they almost lit the room. Her movements were different, too. As the shawl slithered towards the floor it turned into a snake. She caught it without looking and knotted the head and tail firmly around her waist.

"I think he might be able to see my split personality. He definitely saw the mice. Thank goodness we only have to keep him for a few more nights."

71

"We might lose him before that if he goes with me to his aunt's."

Granny flopped down on the sofa and stroked the snake's head. "Don't worry about that. I'll put a jinx on his porridge tomorrow to stop him leaving."

Rexus sighed. "He saved my life, Granny. You won't kill him, will you?"

"That depends on the spell working first time, but if it does, then he can live for all I care."

Chapter Five

Werewolf in Love

Timms hated the law, it was dangerous. Bullfighting would be safer, he was certain of that. He'd been shown into the library and Valentyna had pounced on him the moment he'd said the family couldn't have the money without proof of Vlad's death. The anti-vampire protection seemed to be working, keeping his neck safe from tooth attack, but not from strangulation. Valentyna, wearing leather gloves, shook him until his brain felt like mush.

"Why won't you tell us the bleedin' rhyme?" she screeched. "Oh drat, so sorry. I forgot my exalted position in society for a moment." Her voice returned to its usual cultured tones, but the shaking continued. "Vlad must be dead.

There is no way the puny little wimp could have survived in the forest."

Timms' legs waggled like limp lettuce. He was sure he'd never be able to stand still once the vampire let go of him. Without warning, Valentyna flung him to the ground and he scrambled towards the door, but she flew between him and freedom.

"Where do you think you're going, little worm?"

She appeared to grow another six inches as she reached down and lifted him to his feet.

"My dear Timms," she said, "you can't leave us now. Why not sit down over there on that wonderfully soft, comfortable couch and tell us again why my husband can't have his inheritance."

Timms tottered across the room and collapsed on the sofa. He looked at Valentyna with growing respect. He hadn't thought it possible, but here was someone even more intimidating than Mrs Timms.

"Um, er, um … er," he began.

He could see Valentyna clenching and unclenching her fists. Fear of what she might do if he didn't explain, loosened his tongue.

"It's the law. There has to be proof that the

present owner is dead. It's possible that the werewolves did kill him, but unless you can prove it, you will have to wait for seven years before you can inherit," he said in a rush, glad that he'd finally managed to get the words out.

Valentyna stared at him without saying a word. Timms' nerves, already frayed, gave out and he began to babble.

"It's the law, you see. I'm a lawyer and I have to do what the law says. That's why I'm called a lawyer. I can't break the law because it's the law and ..." he broke off as the vampire floated towards him with glaring red eyes.

"Fine, proof, you need proof, you shall have it," she said, seizing him and pushing him towards the door. "We'll send for you when we have proof."

He fled along the corridor, hardly daring to believe he'd escaped once more.

Valentyna slammed the door and shuddered. Any more of the man's babble and she'd have shaken him until his head fell off. For the time being they needed him alive, but once they had the money and the castle, she'd take great delight in drinking the idiot dry.

Viktor crossed the room and kissed her neck.

"Calm down, my delight. It appears, my sweet nightstar, that until we can produce Vlad's body, the lawyer won't tell us the rhyme. I think we'll have to venture once more into the forest and find the hupyre's remains. I'll call the children."

* * *

Valentyna watched from the upper landing as Boris flew around the vast hall knocking over suits of armour and smashing ornaments. Gretchen screamed and kicked the sofa.

She knew why her children were so enraged. They'd swooped low over Dank Forest, backwards and forwards for hour after dreary hour. At first the twins had seen it as good fun, after all they were hoping to find Vlad's body, or at least the bits the werewolves had left. But when they'd grown bored and had wanted to find a villager to torture, she had said no. Usually she encouraged them to have as much fun as possible, but it was better not to upset the villagers until their position at the castle was secure. Vampire law was funny about invitations and ownership. They needed to be established as owners before facing down a mob, or who knew what might go wrong? By the time they'd returned to the castle, all of them were in foul moods.

"I wish we'd never come to this stinking castle," Boris moaned. "I hate this place. I bet all the old gang back home are out flying formations and hunting humans, but we have to stay in this dreary old dump where we're not even allowed to torture the servants."

Gretchen stopped kicking the sofa.

"Do you think we'll have to stay here forever? I hate it, too. I don't know why Mama loves this rotten castle so much."

"Shall I tell you, my babies?"

Both of them jumped. Valentyna drifted down the stairs smiling. It was the kind of sabre-toothed smile that made rats run for cover. She, too, was fed up with searching for Vlad's body and had suggested to Viktor a few delightful ways of persuading Timms to give them what they wanted. But he had refused, saying he'd be happier knowing Vlad wouldn't be coming back in a few years to reclaim his possessions. Sometimes she found herself wishing Viktor was just a little less *proper*. She'd fallen for him because of his place in society, but there were times when she longed for him to bend some vampire rules – like the one about not killing other vampires. She'd have happily murdered the hupyre and spat out the bits to prove to Timms that Vlad was dead.

"Your beloved papa was born here nearly five centuries ago. In my opinion, he should have inherited this castle after your grandpapa had his unfortunate little accident. Really, you'd have thought the old man would have known better than to take up the javelin at his age. He'd almost reached his thousandth birthday!"

"What happened?" asked Gretchen.

"Grandpapa threw the javelin and one of the servants threw it back. Remarkably accurate he was, too." She shuddered. "Grandpapa died of a broken heart."

She floated across the room and reclined gracefully on a velvet chaise longue.

"Ilya, Vlad's father, was the elder and had shown no signs of settling down and raising a family of his own. We would have waited for him to die at the hands of the locals, or even a bounty hunter, but then he married that …

that … human," she spat. "And they produced a … a," she shuddered, "a *hupyre*. Well, that was too much. And that's why I decided, that is, *we* decided to come and take over. Imagine proud Vlad the Impaler, scourge of Magdorovia, being succeeded by a little rat who can't stop wheezing at the thought of blood. Vlad the Inhaler would be a laughing stock in the vampire world and that we couldn't allow."

"Where is Vlad's father?" asked Boris.

"As dead as a vampire can ever be. We don't need to worry about him popping up again," Valentyna said. "It's just a pity we didn't know about this stupid rhyme, or we could have found out about it before we had Ilya removed."

"So what happens if Vlad is never found?" asked Gretchen.

"The lawyer says we have to wait for seven years before your father can inherit, but I'm not prepared to wait that long. Either we find Vlad soon or the lawyer will be spending some time in the dungeons – and you two can decide which torture instruments will work best to make him recite the secret verse."

* * *

Vlad woke, confused and frightened. Where was he? The bed was small and this place had none of his things in it. Shivering, he remembered his horrible dream of werewolves, bounty hunters and strange old ladies. Then he heard Rexus' voice downstairs and realised his nightmare hadn't been a dream after all. He was in Rexus' bedroom. He looked at the clock. Ten o'clock! He'd slept nearly the whole morning.

He got up and crossed to the small washbasin. Splashing water on his face made him feel a bit better, but when he looked in the mirror he realised he must still be pretty tired. As he peered, his face gradually faded until he could see the reflection of the wall behind him. He shut his eyes and shook his head. When he looked again, his face showed in the mirror as clear as anything. *What on earth was happening to him?* He quickly straightened his hair and went downstairs.

"Hello, my little one," Granny Entwhistle said. "You settle yourself down there next to Rexus while I get you something to eat. You'd like that, wouldn't you?"

"Yes please," Vlad said.

The mention of food made his stomach

grumble so loudly he could feel his face catching fire. He went and sat next to Rexus on the sofa, hoping no one else had heard the noise. Rexus was dressed in a suit and looked completely different to the night before. Vlad would never have guessed he was a werewolf.

Granny called out to say their food was ready and they went into the kitchen. She placed a steaming bowl in front of each of them.

"Porridge oats," she said, "and help yourself to the Dank Forest honey."

"Dank Forest honey?" Vlad asked. "Proper Dank Forest honey?"

"Is there any other kind?" Granny said with a grin.

Vlad began to shake. Dank Forest honey tasted of whatever your favourite flavour might be. Normally he loved it, but he couldn't rid his mind of his strange desire for blood. Then he remembered his reflection disappearing. What if his vampire side was getting stronger?

"Go on, Vlad," said Rexus. "Take some."

Vlad reached out and spooned a big dollop onto his porridge. It looked delicious, but what if it tasted of blood? He did his best to think of his favourite fruit. Big ripe juicy peaches, that's what he wanted it to taste of. He dipped his spoon in the porridge and honey mix and brought it to his lips. He closed his eyes and sucked the honey from the spoon.

"Well?" asked Rexus. "What flavour did you go for? Mine tastes like chocolate."

"Peaches," Vlad said with a massive grin. "My honey tastes of peaches."

He scooped up the porridge with gusto, clearing the bowl in no time at all. Putting down the spoon, he stood up.

"Thank you so much for letting me stay here and for feeding me, Granny," he said.

"You're very welcome, Vlad. If your aunt won't help, then you must come back here and we'll see if we can come up with another plan. Stay on the edge of the forest, though. Don't go into the village unless the coast is clear."

Granny opened the front door and sunlight flooded in. Vlad took a step towards the door and fell to his knees screaming.

"Argh, it hurts. It hurts. Shut the door."

He heard the door slam and the pain, which had sent invisible knives into every part of his body, disappeared.

"What happened?" Rexus asked.

"I don't know. It felt like red hot needles. As if I was melting. But why? I don't understand.

I've been out in daylight loads of times. My mum made sure I got used to it from the time I was a baby. What's going on with me?"

He felt the familiar tightening of his chest and reached for his inhaler, but it wasn't in his pocket. Getting to his feet, he searched for it.

"I can't … can't … breathe. Help me, please, can't … find … inhaler," he gasped, patting and double-checking every pocket.

"I've got just the thing to help you with your asthma, Vlad," said Granny Entwhistle. She disappeared into the kitchen and came back with a tiny canvass bag. "The herbs in there will help you."

Vlad held the bag to his nose and inhaled deeply. The sweet fragrance filled his lungs and his breath became less ragged. It didn't work as fast as his inhaler, but it worked. His eyes filled with tears of relief.

"Thank you, that's amazing. How did you know what I needed?"

"Because I'm good with herbs. I just seem to know which ones cure which ailment. That's why the villagers call me a witch. It doesn't stop them coming out here to ask for help, though," she said. "I think you'd best stay here with me, Vlad, until it gets dark. Rexus can go and talk to your aunt."

Vlad was too shaken by what had happened to argue.

Rexus smiled reassuringly. "I'll go now, Vlad. I don't know how long I'll be, but I'll get back as quickly as I can. If I take George, I'll get there in no time."

Granny and Rexus went out to saddle the donkey. Vlad sat on the stairs and tried to work out was happening. Was he turning into a full vampire? He jumped to his feet and raced up to the bedroom. Almost too scared to look, he forced himself to stare into the mirror.

It was worse than he'd feared. His reflection was virtually transparent.

***

Rexus waited until he and Granny reached the barn before speaking.

"How did you know he'd need that herb bag?"

"Because when I hugged him last night I lifted the inhaler from his pocket. Every time he breathes in the herbs, the porridge jinx strengthens. He'll be convinced he can't go out in daylight. It will add to the image spell I put in his food last night," Granny said with a grin. "He won't be able to see his reflection at all by tonight."

"I feel sorry for him."

"Rexus, don't be stupid. We finally have a hupyre in our grasp. How many spells have I tried with substitutes? None of them worked, not even when I mixed human and vampire blood."

"At least since you did that last spell I can stand upright and talk during full moon."

"And if I do it right with the hupyre's blood you'll never have to worry about full moons ever again. Right, off you go. Just wander around in the forest for a few hours and then come back," Granny said.

"No. I've been thinking that I really should go to his aunt."

"Why?"

"So that he'll have somewhere safe to go afterwards. There will be an afterwards for him, won't there?"

Rexus didn't like the way Granny looked everywhere but at him.

"Granny, he will survive, won't he?"

"What? Oh, yes, of course he will. Go on then, do your good deed and find his aunt, but you'll have to think up a reason to explain why you can't deliver him to her for a few days."

"No. I think it's easier to say I'll bring him over tonight and think of a reason for the delay when I really take him in a couple of days."

Rexus climbed on George and headed into the forest with a wave.

A few hours later he tied George to a tree on the edge of the forest and strolled into Malign village. He'd never been there before and wasn't sure where to begin looking for Vlad's Aunt Elsabetta. Then he saw the pub and thought that would be the best place to ask. Glancing up at the *Ye Olde Stake House* sign he realised he needed to be careful which questions he asked. The landlord might know Vlad's aunt was related to the vampires.

He walked into the pub and tried to act casual as he strolled up to the bar. He could feel the landlord's eyes watching his every movement from under thick, bushy eyebrows. All conversation ceased and the place went completely quiet. It was obvious, from the way he was being stared at, that strangers were rare in Malign.

Hundreds of crosses lined the walls. Fat bulbs of garlic hung from every beam. A large bowl of water stood on the counter. Hanging above it was a sign.

BEFORE DIPPING YOUR HANDS IN YOUR POCKET, PLEASE DIP THEM IN HOLY WATER.

Rexus obliged and swished his hands. A collective sigh filled the room. He grinned, toying with the idea of pretending to be in agony, but thought better of it when he saw the pile of sharpened stakes in the corner.

The landlord bustled up with a welcoming smile.

"Yes, young sir, what can I get for you?"

"I'll have a half pint of lemonade, please," Rexus said returning the smile.

"You're a stranger to these parts," the landlord said, putting the drink down on the counter.

"I am at that. Do you know this village well?"

"I was born and bred here. Albert Grundig's my name and I've been landlord of Ye Olde Stake House for more than thirty years. And my father was landlord before me, and *his* father before him, and *his* father before him. Why do you ask?"

"I'm looking for a job. I wondered if maybe you could point me in the direction of someone who might need a strong person to cut logs and generally fetch and carry."

The landlord began showing off his knowledge of every inhabitant of the village, and he rambled on for an eternity before getting around to Vlad's aunt.

"Then there's Elsabetta Deerling, but she's one to avoid. You don't want to be offering to work for her if you've any sense."

"Why not?" asked Rexus.

The landlord leant forward and whispered: "She's kin to the vampires up at the castle, that's why. Her sister married one of them. You can't trust anyone who has owt to do with the vampires. They've been preying on this village for hundreds of years. The last Count was the worst of the lot because he pretended he'd given up his blood sucking ways. We all believed him, too, and then he attacked without warning. You'd best stay away from Elsabetta Deerling, that's my advice."

"Well, I'd better make sure not to go anywhere near her house. Can you tell me which one it is? I don't want to end up there by mistake," Rexus said trying to look horrified.

Ten minutes later, Rexus said goodbye with the landlord's good wishes ringing in his ears.

That had turned out easier than he'd expected. He now had the exact location of Elsabetta Deerling's house.

He walked through the narrow streets, feeling pretty pleased with himself and carefully noting the landmarks Albert Grundig had told him to look out for. He passed the wishing well, turned left and kept going until he reached the covered market and then turned right. Elsabetta's house was the middle property in a row of large town houses, all with massive wrought-iron balconies standing out from the upper floors. The road was so narrow the balconies from each side almost met in the middle. He knew he'd reached the right house by the tubs of bright red geraniums outside – Albert's final landmark.

He knocked on the door and a young girl opened it.

"Could I please speak to Elsabetta Deerling?" he asked, trying not to stare at the sweetest heart-shaped face and cutest little turned-up nose he'd ever seen. Violet eyes and hair the colour of wild honey swam in front of his blurred vision.

Movement from behind the girl brought the moment to a close.

"Who's there, Lisette?" called a commanding voice.

"Someone for you, madam," said the girl.

"Well, who is it, child?"

Before the girl could answer, Rexus stepped around her into the entrance hall, almost colliding with an ornately carved cask full of umbrellas and walking sticks. He blinked in surprise as his reflection, and that of the woman, came back at him, repeated tenfold from several mirrors. The woman peered into a mirror and tweaked one of the blonde curls piled high on her head. She spotted Rexus and whirled round.

"What are you doing in my house? Get out! Lisette, what do you mean by letting ruffians in?"

"I'm not a ruffian. I've come about your nephew, ma'am. I'm sorry to intrude."

His words didn't have the effect he's hoped for. The woman's face hardened. She was nowhere near as tall as Rexus, but she seemed to be looking down her pointy nose at him. Slim and immaculately made up, wearing an expensive-looking silk dress, she made Rexus feel as though he should have gone to the tradesmen's entrance.

"I don't have a nephew, young man. I think you should leave."

Rexus stood his ground. "But you do have a nephew, you know you do, and he needs your help. He's escaped from the castle and is desperate for a safe place to hide."

Elsabetta frowned. "Escaped? You have five minutes to convince me I have a nephew worth saving. Five minutes, that's all, and then you leave."

She turned her back and walked across the marble floor. He'd never been in such a grand house. The entrance hall was almost as big as Granny's cottage.

Rexus followed her into the drawing room. This room was definitely *bigger* than Granny's cottage. Or maybe it just seemed that way because it was also full of mirrors reflecting the room back over and over. Rexus was mesmerised by his own reflection going on into infinity.

"When you've quite finished admiring yourself perhaps you'll tell me what you mean by barging in here like this. I told you that you only had five minutes and I meant it. You've wasted two of them already."

Rexus jumped, pulled himself together and

spoke as quickly as he could, telling Elsabetta everything that had happened to Vlad.

Elsabetta gasped. "My poor sister," she said, her eyes filling with tears. "I know I was angry with Katerina, and I still don't agree with mixed species marriages, but her son is my flesh and blood. Where is he now?"

"Somewhere safe," answered Rexus. "Somewhere Viktor and Valentyna will never think to look."

"Well, you did right to tell me about his problems. You must bring him to me and I'll take care of him. He's all the family I have left in the world."

"Yes, all right, but I don't think he should risk being seen by the villagers. I'll bring him over tonight. Where will you hide him? He can't stay here with you. It's the first place his aunt and uncle will look, I think," Rexus said.

At least if I can get him to safety afterwards I won't feel so bad about Granny using his blood, Rexus thought. He liked Vlad. If only he wasn't a hupyre.

Elsabetta smiled. "Your concern does you credit. Don't you worry; I'm going to take very good care of Vlad. I'll take him to another village, far from here. He'll never need to fear anything ever again."

Rexus got up to go, eager to see the serving girl before he left. He bowed low to Elsabetta. As he stepped into the hall he heard the rustle of a skirt and footsteps lightly tapping over the marble, like someone running, but trying not to make a noise. He walked towards the door and there she was, looking shy. Rexus couldn't help hoping she'd run there especially to see him.

He wanted to tell her he'd be back later, but somehow his tongue had become glued to the roof of his mouth and all that came out was a muffled grunt. Embarrassed, he half smiled and, tried to look nonchalant as well as keeping his eyes on his dream girl. He forgot about the umbrella stand and walked straight into it. The stand toppled over and so did he. He scrambled to his feet.

"Urh, um," he mumbled.

Face blushing fit to catch fire, he fled. He'd just reached the end of the street when he heard footsteps behind him. He stopped and turned to see his dream girl running towards him.

"I have something to tell you, please wait," she yelled.

He stood, heart pounding with joy. She'd

run after him. She must like him after all.

She reached his side and gasped for breath, then spoke: "Don't bring your friend to Elsabetta. She's in league with the vampires from the castle."

Chapter Six

Confusing Us, he say ... Ommm

Vlad steeled himself to open the front door of the cottage. While Granny was busy in the kitchen, he'd crept out of the sitting room into the tiny hallway and tried to face the daylight six times. Each time had been more painful than the last. But he couldn't bear the thought of his vampire side taking over. He had to try again. As he reached for the door, his hand shook so much he wondered if he'd be able to grip the handle. What if he died this time when the daylight hit him? His hand dropped to his side. He couldn't do it. He just couldn't.

"Come on, Vlad," he whispered, "don't be a wimp. It's face daylight or drink blood for the next thousand years. Besides, it's nearly dusk, so maybe it won't hurt as much."

He reached out again, but before his hand connected with the handle, the door flew open and Rexus rushed in, slamming the door behind him and leaning against it.

"What is it, Rexus? What's wrong? Were you chased by Skinner and Bones?"

Rexus didn't answer, but shook his head and held up his hand as if asking Vlad to wait. Then he howled. Loud screaming howls that filled the cottage and echoed back off the walls. Fur sprouted from his face and the backs of his hands. He ripped off his jacket and shirt, dropped to his knees, and clutched his head.

"Rexus, Rexus, what can I do to help?" Vlad yelled, but the creature ignored him.

Granny came running from the kitchen. "It's all right, Vlad," she yelled over the ever-increasing noise. "Rexus takes a while to change. He must have just caught the first light of tonight's moon. Come through to the kitchen with me until he's finished."

Vlad took one last look at Rexus writhing on the floor, wishing there was something he could do.

Rexus looked up. "Goooooooooooo," he howled.

Vlad followed Granny to the kitchen. The

howls continued for another five minutes, punctuated by grunts. Then silence filled the air and Vlad heard Rexus' footsteps approaching.

"Sorry about that, Vlad. I almost didn't get back in time. I hate changing in the forest because I never know what's about that might attack me when I'm weak like that." He smiled through fearsome teeth. "I'm sorry, I have some bad news. Your aunt seemed like a really nice lady and said she'd hide you until you were older. But then, after I'd left, her maid ran after me and said your aunt was the one who told the Malign villagers it was your dad who'd taken the child."

"What? Why would she do that?"

"I don't know, but the maid said you wouldn't be safe there," Rexus said and explained everything that had happened in Malign, including wanting to pretend the holy water had burnt him, but Vlad wasn't in the mood to find it funny.

"This means I don't have anywhere else to go apart from Mary and Joe's. I'd better go tonight."

Granny stood up and bustled over to the range. Vlad again had the strange sensation of there being two people moving as one.

"Here, Vlad," she said as she turned back to him. "Drink this. You need something warm inside you before you set out to cross the forest."

The rich sweet smell of hot chocolate wafted up from the mug and Vlad couldn't resist downing it in one go.

"That was delicious. Thank you, Granny."

"I'm glad you enjoyed it," she said. "I must go and see to the donkeys." She smiled and left the kitchen.

"Rexus," Vlad said. "I tried to go out into daylight while you were away, but I couldn't do it. It hurt too much. You don't think I'm turning into a full vampire, do you?"

"Nah, if you were, you'd want to drink blood. So I wouldn't worry about it."

"But that's exactly why I *am* worried. You know when Skinner …"

Before he could continue, Rexus chuckled.

"What's so funny?"

Rexus grinned at him. "We're like one of those clocks they make in Subversia," he said. "You know, those weather clocks where the troll comes out if it's going to rain and the dragon comes out if the sun is shining."

"Rexus, what are you going on about?"

"Have you not seen them? It's a mechanical device that only lets one figure out at a time. When the other one comes out, the first one has to go in. That's like us. I can go out during the day as a normal human, but you can't. You can come out at night like one, but I can't. If you were a full vampire, night-time would be when you went out hunting for victims. Lucky for us you don't feel the urge to drink blood."

Vlad decided it was best to keep his urges secret. Maybe they'd fade if he didn't confess to anyone.

"Can I ask you something, Rexus?"

"Sure, of course you can. What do you want to know?"

"You know when you found me in the forest? What were you doing?"

"Looking for a special ingredient for Granny."

"Weren't you scared of meeting up with Skinner?"

"I'm always scared of him, Vlad, but I've been searching for years for the right substance and now it's even more important that her spell works."

Vlad could hardly keep his eyes open. The room swayed and Rexus' voice seemed to be coming from further and further away. He forced himself to concentrate on what the werewolf had said.

"Why'sitmore … 'portant?" he asked on a massive yawn.

"Because of golden hair like silk and violet eyes to drown in."

That made no sense at all to Vlad. He shook his head, trying to get rid of the woolly feeling drifting through his brain. "'sthat mean?"

"You must promise not to laugh if I tell you."

"Promisssssssse," Vlad slurred. "Word of a … Malign … teeth go … blunt if … tell a lie."

"It's your aunt's maid. Her name is Lisette."

Vlad's head fell forward. His last thought before he passed out was to wonder how Rexus could have been searching for years for an ingredient to please someone he'd met for the first time today.

Rexus smiled as Granny came back into the kitchen looking like a little old lady. She changed when she saw Vlad fast asleep. The snake hissed as it slithered into place around her neck, its eyes glittering in the candlelight.

"Help me carry him upstairs, Rexus. The

chocolate drug should keep him asleep until this time tomorrow night. And then, a sharp knife, a waning moon and all your worries will be over. No more Mr Werewolf for you."

Rexus stood and helped Granny get Vlad to his feet. He felt like a murderer. Even though Granny had promised not to take more of Vlad's blood than she needed, he wasn't sure how much that really was. If he had to choose between staying a werewolf and Vlad's life, was there really any choice?

***

Gretchen studied the bloodbank housemaid tidying her coffin room. To Gretchen she looked like dinner. Not being able to kill the servants seemed stupid to her. She wondered if she'd get away with drinking this one dry, instead of using her as a snack between meals. They had so many; surely no one would notice one was missing. She crept towards the woman, but as she was about to pounce, the door flew open.

"We're wanted in the library," Boris yelled.

She followed Boris down the stairs, hoping

it didn't mean flying over the stupid forest yet again. She entered the library to find her parents looking delighted.

"We've just had a most interesting visitor," said Valentyna. "It seems Vlad is alive. Your father and I shall pay his aunt a visit tonight – and this time there'll be no mistakes. We'll bring the hupyre back here and keep him captive until the lawyer arrives. After that … well, let's just say your father is finally seeing things from my point of view. He's only a hupyre, so why should the rules about not killing other vampires apply? You two must get everything ready for a family feast. We'll want all the servants lined up to witness the end of their little master's reign."

* * *

Never had a night lasted so long for Elsabetta. Her reflected image usually delighted her, but not this time. Her face looked too white, almost drained of blood. *Don't think of blood draining*. Stray locks of hair had escaped from the fair curls pinned to the top of her head and hung down on one side, making her look slightly demented. Which is what she was, she knew that. Demented from spending a night in the company of Viktor and Valentyna.

Try as she might, she could only see herself and her pretty drawing room reflected in the mirrors. She shuddered and decided that *not* seeing the vampires in the mirrors might almost be worse than seeing them there. She couldn't see their reflection, but they sat on her sofa in the flesh, and refused to leave.

From being one of her favourite places, her sitting room had become the last place she wanted to be. Who wants to share space with vampires? She felt like a specimen under a microscope whenever Viktor or Valentyna looked in her direction. Even the faces of her ornamental china dolls seemed to be sneering.

"Well, where is Vlad?" Viktor asked as he walked over to a mirror and peered into it. "Do I look handsome, my dear Elsabetta? What do you see in these mirrors of yours? You seem to be fascinated by reflections. Are you reflecting on the dangers of lying to us?"

Elsabetta squirmed and held tightly to the garlic cloves hidden in her pockets. She wished Viktor and Valentyna would remain sitting down. Every time they moved, she felt the blood leaving her face. It seemed it would only be a matter of time before it left her body.

"He's coming, he's coming," she answered.

"You keep saying that," Valentyna said, levitating off the sofa and floating across the room. Her eyes glowed red and her incisors seemed longer and sharper than ever.

"But he is coming. I promise he is."

Valentyna drifted closer and Elsabetta scrambled away, edging backwards until she reached the wall and couldn't retreat any further.

"If you've lied to trick us into giving you money, do you know what we'll do?"

With the vampire's face only inches from hers, Elsabetta couldn't move, couldn't think; her brain had turned to slush.

"We'll take every penny back – in blood!" Valentyna sneered.

"He's coming. He is coming. The boy said he'd bring him. Coming, yes, coming. He is, yes, yes, soon, yes. Coming he is," Elsabetta babbled, clinging to the wall to stop herself from collapsing.

"She isn't any fun, Viktor," Valentyna complained. "Stop trying to see yourself and make her do something interesting."

"What would you like her to do, my darkest one? Should she dance for you? Or sing? No? Well maybe she could perform a conjuring trick and *produce my nephew out of thin air*!" he yelled. He took a deep breath. "I refuse to get over-excited; it's bad for my blood pressure. I shall meditate."

In front of Elsabetta's incredulous eyes, the vampire floated to the centre of the room. Suspended in midair, he crossed his legs and put his palms together. His eyes swivelled upwards and a look of calm settled on his face.

"Ommmmmmmmm. Ommmmmmmmm. Ommmmmmmmmm," he chanted.

"Viktor, what in all that is evil are you doing?"

Viktor opened one eye. "I read about it in one of the library books. When humans get upset they calm down by searching for their inner self. Apparently meditating is a required element. It looked like fun, so I'm going to try it." He resumed his position of repose. "Ommmmmmmmmm."

"I hate it when he reads," Valentyna said. "It goes straight to his brain and fries it. There are times when I think his family might be too inbred. So many of the old aristocratic families are, you know, and Viktor's is one of the oldest families of all."

She continued boasting of her high society connections in a singsong voice, with Viktor omming in the background, until Elsabetta thought she would go insane. Eventually, she heard the words she'd thought would never come.

"Viktor, stop that noise and come down. It's time to go."

"Ah, yes, it is almost dawn," Viktor said as he dropped to the ground. "We must fly home to our coffins."

"Shall we kill her first?" Valentyna asked, drifting towards him.

Elsabetta hoped Viktor was too much in tune with his inner vampire to consider it.

"No, she is smothered in protection. We'll just take our money," he said lifting the bag from the table, "and come back when she doesn't expect us. We'll kill her then."

They changed into bats and were gone while Elsabetta was still begging them to spare her.

* * *

Boris and Gretchen ducked as their parents whooshed around over their heads. Viktor and Valentyna dive-bombed ornaments, suits of armour and even their children.

"What do you suppose happened?" Gretchen whispered from behind a sofa.

"I think Vlad must have escaped again," Boris answered as two black shapes whizzed past.

Valentyna changed form and landed.

"It isn't fair," she screeched. "That horrible little hupyre should be dead by now. Ripped to shreds, bled white, sucked dry and neatly laid out to show that stupid lawyer, Tiddles, Times, or whatever his name is."

Immediately she changed back to a bat again and resumed her erratic flying, almost colliding with Viktor, who was coming down to land.

"We need a plan," he snarled at his bemused offspring. "Don't just stand there. Think of a way to entice your half-breed cousin into the open. Keeping all of this," he said, gesturing to the magnificent hall, "depends on us killing the little freak."

He shot upwards to rejoin Valentyna who'd perfected her target diving. The clattering sound of a helmet rolling across the floor signalled a direct hit. The twins shuffled to the window, but Valentyna swooped in their path.

"Don't you dare slope off," she snarled. "Think! Think of a way to find your stupid cousin."

"They should have left the hunt to me," hissed Boris as his mother took off again.

"You?" Gretchen sneered. "You said you'd seen him in the forest and nearly got us eaten by werewolves. Left to you, Vlad will never be found. But if they haven't a clue, how are we supposed to guess?"

"I expect some of those revolting humans who love him so much are hiding him," Boris said.

"You mean that Mary creature who used to be his nurse? He isn't there; Mama has had their hovel watched. I don't see why we can't just bite the lawyer until he gives us the rhyme. Searching for treasure would be more fun than ..." Gretchen ducked as another piece of armour sailed overhead. "More fun than looking for Vlad. Once we find him, he'll be no challenge at all. Imagine being looked after by a load of humans. Anyone would turn out soft."

"I wouldn't," Boris insisted. "But I expect you would. You're just a pathetic girl."

Gretchen's black eyes went wide.

"I've got it. I've got it," she cried. "I know how to trap Vlad."

"You do not," scoffed Boris. "You're just saying that."

"I do, too. You're just cross because you can't think of any good ideas. You're a stupid, useless …"

Valentyna landed next to the twins.

"Yes, Gretchen, he may be all the things you want to say, but if you have a plan, then tell us what it is," she ordered.

By the time Gretchen had finished explaining, even Boris was grinning.

Chapter Seven

Chocolate Flavoured Sleep

Vlad opened his eyes to a darkened room. Where was he? He could remember talking to Rexus about his aunt's maid, but then what happened? He moved to light the candle and a stabbing pain shot through his head, so sharp he almost threw up. His dry mouth screamed at him for water. Moving slowly, keeping his throbbing head as still as possible, he managed to light the candle and look around. Rexus' bedroom! He was back in Rexus' room. How had that happened? Why couldn't he remember?

He had to get up and go downstairs. Had he passed out? Walking gingerly, not moving his head more than he had to, he avoided the bedroom mirror. He had enough to worry about, without finding out he might now have no reflection at all.

He found Granny and Rexus in the kitchen seated at the table. Vlad was surprised to see a human Rexus and felt even more confused.

Granny stood up as Vlad came in and he was sure he saw her hair change to red before it went back to the usual white curls. One side of her shawl lifted and hissed at him. Shaken, he sat at the table and shut his eyes. When he looked again, the shawl was draped around her shoulders as it should be. Now he was hallucinating. Great, that's all he needed.

"I'm sorry," he said. "I have such a headache. Rexus, how come you're not a werewolf?"

"I only turn when the moon is full," he said. "Last night was the final time for this month. Tonight is the first night of the waning moon."

"But … no, that can't be right. How long have I been asleep?"

"Twenty-four hours," said Granny moving to the range. "You fell asleep right here at the table last night, so we carried you up to bed."

"That's right, Vlad," said Rexus. "I expect you were exhausted from everything you've been through."

Vlad heard a hiss from behind and spun round. Granny was turning from the range with a mug in her hand. The shawl slithered around her neck and two staring emerald eyes glittered in the lamplight. As Vlad opened his mouth to warn Granny she had a snake round her neck, it turned back into a shawl and lay innocently around her shoulders.

"I think you could be right," agreed Vlad. "I'm tired enough to see things that aren't there. I must get to Joe and Mary's tonight, but I feel so washed out."

"Drink this," said Granny. "It will keep you warm in the forest."

He lifted the mug and the wonderful chocolate smell made Vlad think of something, but he couldn't quite put his finger on what it was. He knew it was important and to do with drinking the chocolate, but what was it? He put the mug down. His head was aching fit to bust.

"Drink up, Vlad," said Granny, leaning over him with a smile.

She was so close. The room was too stuffy. Rexus looked anxious. Vlad felt sick, but Granny's smile made him want to drink the chocolate more than anything else in the world. He was so thirsty. The drink called to him. He lifted the mug again and brought it to his lips …

Thump!

Thump!

Thump!

Thump!

"Oh my! My door is likely to come off its hinges. Quick," she said, pushing Vlad towards the broom cupboard. "Get in there and stay as silent as a mouse."

She swung the door open and pushed Vlad inside. He stumbled into the gloomy space and pulled the door closed, leaving only the tiniest of cracks for air. Could it be his aunt and uncle? There were voices shouting. It wasn't Viktor or Valentyna, but it *was* a voice he recognised. He decided to sneak out to hear better. Quietly, he opened the door and the light revealed his inhaler on the shelf next to the polish and dusters. Granny must have found it for him. He put it in his pocket and then crept over to listen.

"Calm down and stop yelling," Rexus said. "You'll have a heart attack."

"Okay, okay, I'm sorry," the familiar voice replied. "It's just that I'm desperate. I need an invisibility spell and I need it now! I'll pay you anything. *Anything!*"

"You must be mistaken," said Granny in a soft tone. "I'm not a witch. I'm just a poor little old lady living quietly with her grandson."

"That's not what Mrs Pendleton sez. She sez she asked for a spell to stop her husband cheating on her. Now he follows her everywhere. Can't take his eyes off her, she sez. He even sits up and begs if she tells him to. We all calls him puppy Pendleton."

"Very well," said Granny, "but I can't do anything for you tonight. I shall be very busy later and need time to prepare. You'll have to leave and come back tomorrow."

"*Tomorrow?* It'll be too late by then. The vampires have taken my Mary prisoner and they's going to kill her. Please, missus, please give me an invisibility spell so's I can rescue her."

Vlad came out of the kitchen. "Joe? Is it really you? But what's that you said about Mary?"

"Master Vlad!" Joe exclaimed. "What in all that is dank are you doing here? Oh, thank goodness. Now my Mary will be saved. Your aunt and uncle have Mary and said I had to find you or they'd kill her. I had no idea where to look, so came to get me a spell instead, but please, master Vlad, you must come with me to save my Mary." The big man's tears fell like a waterfall. "She's done everything for you since you was a baby. Youse gotta help her now. Youse gotta!"

Vlad swallowed hard and wished he felt braver. "Of course, I'll go with you, Joe," he said, forcing the words out.

"I don't think you should go, Vlad," said Granny. "You're in no fit state to face your aunt and uncle."

"I can't leave my Mary in danger," Joe wailed.

"I have to go," Vlad said. "I couldn't bear it if anything happened to her."

"All I'm saying is we should think about what our options are," Granny insisted.

"Do we have any?" Vlad asked.

"Yes, come on into the sitting room and let's talk it out," Granny said pulling Joe inside and slamming the front door.

The room felt packed with all four of them in there, especially as Joe paced round and round, far too agitated to stand still and talk. Vlad followed him, but his shorter strides meant he had to jog to keep up. Joe stopped suddenly and Vlad jogged into his back.

"What are you doing, master Vlad?" Joe sighed. "Get up off the floor now. This is no time to play the fool."

Vlad scrambled to his feet.

"Do stop pacing, you two," Granny said. "You're making me feel dizzy. Sit down and listen, I've worked out a plan."

"Thank goodness," said Joe. "They might have tortured her to death by now."

"They won't do that," soothed Granny. "They'll keep her alive for a day or two yet. They don't know how long it might take you to find Vlad. The way I see it, if Vlad goes back with you, his family will find a way to kill him and they'll most probably kill Mary as well, just for the fun of it."

"But if I don't go, they'll kill Mary anyway," Vlad said.

He felt his chest tighten. He had to stay calm. Mary depended on him!

"Listen to me," Granny insisted. "I think Rexus should go to Malign village and force Vlad's aunt Elsabetta to tell the truth about that child's murder and her part in the uprising to the landlord at the pub. From what Rexus told us, he seems to be the type of person the villagers would follow. He can raise an army and attack the vampires in the castle."

"But what about me?" asked Vlad.

"You must stay here with me," said Granny. "Joe can go back and tell your aunt and uncle that he couldn't find you, but that he knows of someone who knows where you are and that person will bring you to them."

"I don't like that idea," said Joe, miserably.

"Nor me," said Vlad. "They might be so angry they'll kill Mary."

"Well, as it's the only idea anyone has come up with," Granny interrupted, "and neither of you two can think of a better plan, I think that's what should happen."

Vlad hunched his shoulders. He didn't like Granny's idea one little bit, but it didn't matter. He'd thought of a plan of his own, but he wasn't going to tell anyone about it. Granny seemed determined he should stay in the cottage, so maybe she'd try to stop him. He just wished his head didn't feel as fuzzy. He was having trouble thinking straight, but convinced himself his plan would work.

Joe frowned. "I'm rubbish at lying," he said. "Mary always knows when I've been telling porkies. I'm not sure I could convince them nasty folk of anything."

"But Joe," Rexus said, "all you have to say is that you couldn't find Vlad. Tell them you found me instead and I know where Vlad is."

"Yes, that's all very well, but what if they ups and kills my Mary anyway? Thirteen years we've been married," he said.

Everyone stared at Joe.

"What?" he asked. "Why are you looking like that?"

"You said *the* word, Joe," Vlad explained. "You said the number between twelve and fourteen."

"I knows I did. I'm not stupid. Thirt …"

He stopped as Granny stood up and glared at him. "Don't you dare say that word in my cottage. Don't you dare! Right, the best way for you to keep your wife safe is for Vlad's family to believe he'll be arriving at any moment. I suggest you leave right now and go back to the castle. Tell them Vlad is on his way."

Joe sighed. "I'm sorry. I didn't know I shouldn't say thirt … that number. I'll go back to the castle. I still don't like it, but I'll do it. Please raise the villagers as quick as you can, Rexus."

"Good," Granny said. "The sooner you both set out the better. Rexus, I need you to come straight back here once your part is done."

Joe, Granny and Rexus went outside. Vlad drew deep breaths of fresh air to clear the fuzzy cloud from his brain. His mouth was still so dry. He remembered he'd been about to drink the chocolate when Joe had hammered on the door.

Vlad went to the kitchen and lifted the mug from the table. He was so very thirsty. He brought it to his lips. Once again he had that strange feeling that a memory was trying to force its way to the surface. There was something he should remember. Something to do with the hot chocolate. But what?

By the time Granny came back from helping Rexus to saddle George, Vlad was sitting at the kitchen table with the empty mug in front of him. He looked up as Granny came in and peered at her with barely open eyes.

"I'm so … sleeeeeepy. Tired, Granny. Soooooooooo tired."

"Why don't you go up to bed, Vlad? You might as well rest until Rexus gets back."

Vlad lurched to his feet. Swaying, he clutched the back of the chair. By the time he reached the hall, he was on his knees and had to crawl up the stairs. Using the wall, he pulled himself upright and staggered to the bedroom. Dragging himself inside, he shut the door and collapsed on the bed.

Chapter Eight

Granny Sharpens Up

Mary stood in the centre of her cell, as far from the dungeon walls as she could get. The stench from the green slime running down the stonework made her heave. A long granite slab, suspended from the wall opposite the solid iron door, was the only form of furniture. A guttering candle on the floor barely illuminated one corner of the gloom, but it was enough to see the army of spiders scuttling to and fro on giant webs.

Her legs trembled with the effort of staying upright. She swayed from side to side, totally exhausted. It was no good, she had to lie down. She staggered towards the hard bed and climbed onto it. Shivering, she tried to find a comfortable spot, but the cold stone pressed into her bones. Lying next to the slime-covered walls, all she could do was put her hand over her nose and try not to breathe in the rancid smell.

If only she'd listened to Joe and moved away from their cottage. He'd said she was in danger, but oh no, she'd thought she knew best. But her dear, sweet Joe had been right all along. It had been easy for the vampires to capture her. It was too late to think about that now, though. She wondered where Joe was and prayed he'd find a way to rescue her.

A key scraped in the lock and the door creaked open. Mary was blinded by the light from a lantern flooding the room. Was it Joe?

Instead of the voice she longed to hear, Valentyna's sneering tone rang out.

"Isn't my beautiful Gretchen clever? She knew Vlad would turn himself in to save you. He's stupid and sickly, like a typical human."

Mary staggered to her feet. As her eyes adjusted to the light, she looked around, expecting to see Vlad in the vampire's clutches.

"Where is he? What have you done with him?"

Valentyna's eyes glowed red. "Are you worried about little Vlad? Isn't that sweet, children? She's concerned for the hupyre's safety. We don't have him yet, but I should imagine your lump of a husband is on his way back with him right at this moment. What a tasty feast you and Greening will make. You're both plump enough to last for almost an entire night."

Her hand flashed out and she tried to rip the cross from Mary's neck, but the twitching fingers couldn't quite close on it.

"You don't like that, do you?" Mary tried to sneer, but her words came out as a whimper.

"When the time comes to kill you, I shall make one of the servants remove your pathetic jewellery. How can you possibly care about that wheezing hupyre? You deserve to die for having such poor taste."

"Oh please, please don't hurt him," Mary begged. "I've cared for Vlad since he was a baby. I love him, as if he were my own."

Valentyna continued as if Mary hadn't spoken. "My husband found a book in the library saying it's not against our code to kill a hupyre, as long as we don't drink from him. So we'll have to cut his throat instead. It seems a waste of a good meal, but Viktor is so old-school about these things. It comes from his aristocratic lineage, you know. We've sent for the lawyer to view Vlad's body," Valentyna gloated and drifted closer. "It's all going to work out perfectly. But if your useless husband fails to return with Vlad by tomorrow night, we shall drink you anyway. Very, very slowly."

Boris tugged Valentyna's arm. Mary wondered at the look of glee on his face, and nearly fainted when she heard why he looked so cheerful.

"Mama, it's boring waiting for Vlad. Can't Gretchen and I play catch with her?"

"Why not? You'd like to play a game with my beautiful children, wouldn't you, Mary?" she taunted.

Gretchen whispered something in Boris' ear and pirouetted away. He roared with laughter as she danced frenziedly around the room. Mary couldn't drag her eyes away from the girl, as she performed complicated dance moves.

Then Mary felt a cold blade touch the back of her neck, followed by a sharp tug on her neck chain. Too late, she realised Boris had crept behind her while she'd been watching his sister. Her precious crucifix fell to the dungeon floor. Boris pushed her to one side, lifted the chain on his knife and flicked it out of the cell into the corridor.

"*Now* we can play," he grinned. "Come on, Gretchen. Let's go."

Boris dragged Mary screaming from the dungeon and carried her down the long corridors leading to the back of the castle. She clung to door handles and torch holders as she passed them, but each time she got a grip, Gretchen forced her fingers open.

"No point in putting up a fight,
vampires always rule the night," Gretchen sang.

They came to the end of the tunnel and emerged into the night. Boris let Mary go and she fell to her knees.

"Please," she begged. "Please don't hurt me."

"Oh we won't *hurt* you," said Boris as he transformed into a grinning bat. "We're just going to have some fun with you."

Gretchen changed next, twirling her silky batwings and pirouetting into the air.

"Come on, Boris. I'm waiting," she called.

He grabbed Mary by her collar, knocking the breath from her as he flew upwards, high above the jagged rocks.

"Are you ready, Mary?" he yelled over the

roar of the sea crashing onto the rocks far below. With a grin, he let her go.

"Noooooooooooooooooooooooooooo," she screamed as the waves and sharp rocks rushed up to meet her.

With only inches to spare before she was speared on the vicious points, Viktor arrived from nowhere, swept her up and carried her back inside. As he strode along the corridors with Mary over his shoulder both twins yelled at him to give them back their toy. Finally, he reached the dungeons and restored Mary to the safety of her cell.

"Papa, that's not fair," shrieked Gretchen. "Mama said we could play."

"Now look, children," Viktor said. "There's plenty of time for playing later, but for now she must stay in the dungeon. Your dear mother overlooked one little thing – if the nurse is dead we lose our best weapon against your cousin."

"Well, I hope we don't have to wait too long," Gretchen moaned. "It's such fun when the humans scream."

"It always is, my pretty one," agreed Viktor. "You can play with her for days if you wish, but not until Vlad has been dealt with."

Mary sprawled across the dungeon floor as Viktor threw her in. She looked up as the massive iron door closed, shutting her in, but also, to her relief, keeping the twins out. She heard the key turning in the lock, followed by the tinkling sound of it hanging on the hook outside her cell. She crawled to her feet, staggered across the floor and slumped on the hard bed. She tried not to cry, but couldn't stop the tears from falling. All three of them would die, her, Joe and Vlad, and there wasn't a thing she could do to prevent it happening.

* * *

Thump! Thump, thump, thump-thump! Thump! Thump, thump, thump-thump! Thump! Thump, thump, thump-thump!

Timms jumped up and dragged the curtains closed around his four-poster bed. He trembled so much his nightcap fell askew and covered one eye. Determined banging at the door during the hours of darkness could only mean another summons to the castle.

He tried to convince himself his imagination was playing tricks on him and succeeded quite well until the bed curtains swept to one side and Mrs Timms' big puffy face appeared.

"Are you deaf, Timms?" she bellowed. "Someone has been hammering on the door for ages. What's wrong with you?"

He pushed his nightcap away from his eyes and peered at his wife. Hair curlers bulged under a bright green scarf. She wore her dressing gown like a soldier's greatcoat, ready for battle at a moment's notice. Her face carried its usual stern expression and Timms felt ill. She was going to start shouting at him. He touched his neck and winced. The bruises were vivid reminders of his last visit to the castle. Fear of his wife battled with his terror of the vampires.

"I, um, I, um," he stammered.

"I um, I *um*," she mimicked. "What does that mean? I do wish you wouldn't babble, Timms. There's someone at the door and if you don't go and find out who it is I shall have to get *angry*."

These dreadful words sent Timms' heart into a fluttering frenzy. Mrs Timms angry should not be ignored, but the vampires' sharp fangs glinted in his memory. He shifted his position on the bed. Maybe if he held his shoulders back and sounded determined, she might listen to him.

"I, um, I think it's a call for me to go to the castle, Mrs Timms, my, um, dearest."

"Well, if so," she raged, "I hope you're going to take better care of your clothes on this visit, Timms. The last time you went you managed to get your jacket all creased around the lapels."

"I did explain that to you, dearest. The, um, female vampire treated me very roughly."

Should he tell her again the way Valentyna had attacked him? He decided not to bother. Mrs Timms had no imagination whatsoever. He felt life couldn't be more unfair. Why should he have to choose between being attacked by vampires or facing an angry Mrs Timms? There was so little difference between two such dire fates.

Thump! *Bang.* Thump. *Bang.* Thump, thump-thump! *Bang.*

"Now see what you've done! Our neighbours are banging on the walls in protest. Do try to be more of a man, Timms."

Shivering, Timms went downstairs to receive his summons.

* * *

Joe rushed back through the forest towards the castle, but slowed for the final few yards, still trying to work out exactly what to say to the vampires. He found himself listening for screams, convinced he could hear Mary calling. He'd worked at the castle ever since Mary's mistress had married the previous Count, but never before had it appeared so threatening. The torches lighting the drawbridge cast more shadows than light and the turrets, usually welcoming beacons, were in darkness. The massive structure loomed above him like his worst nightmare.

He crossed the drawbridge and entered the outer courtyard, his trembling legs carrying him towards the main building. Four figures swooped gracefully overhead and landed on the steps. The family returned to human form and none of them looked happy.

"Where is the boy?" Valentyna demanded. "Why have you come back without him?"

"I ... I ... I couldn't f ... find him." Every fibre in Joe's body trembled.

"Do you *want* your wife to die?" she taunted,

rising above him, eyes glowing like hot embers.

Joe wanted to run, but his legs refused to move.

"I … I couldn't find him, but…"

"Oh, I've just about 'ad enough of this. Kill 'im," she screeched.

Boris and Gretchen leapt to the air, batwings instantly unfolding. Joe snapped his eyes shut, his brain melting at the thought of dying.

"Wait!" a voice boomed.

Joe opened one eye. Viktor stood between him and the twins.

"Patience, children," he said, raising his hand. "Valentyna, don't be so hasty, my dear. You really should start reading with me. The ancient teachers say that waiting for a pleasant event increases the enjoyment when it arrives. Besides, we need to find out what he knows. Children, take him to the dungeon and we'll interrogate him there."

Boris returned to bat form and lifted Joe with ease, carrying him into the castle.

"Wait for me," screeched Gretchen. "I don't see why you should have all the fun."

They dragged him into the castle and descended the steep stone steps. Gretchen tried to snatch Joe from Boris and he was pulled between the two like a chicken's wishbone. As his head bobbed up and down, he caught sight of Viktor and Valentyna floating along behind.

"See how strong and merciless they are, my dark one," said Valentyna.

Joe, too terrified to think, let alone speak, didn't share Valentyna's delight in her children. Viktor's reply seemed to come from a long way off and he realised he was close to passing out. He pictured Mary and forced himself to stay awake.

"Yes, my deadly nightshade, they remind me of you. They seem to have inherited the worst of both of us. True evil is so delightful to behold. Did I tell you about the great Confusingus? It was from him I learned to meditate. I do wish you'd join me."

"Would I have to make that ridiculous noise?"

Joe couldn't make any sense of their conversation and prayed that meditating didn't involve torturing him. The twins carried him deep under the castle and finally stopped outside one of the cells. Viktor lifted the key from its hook and opened the door.

"Throw him in," Valentyna ordered.

Joe sprawled forward, sliding across the

rough stone floor. His head thumped against the wall and he passed out.

When he came to, he felt gentle hands helping him to rise and realised with relief it was Mary – still alive!

"Oh Joe, are you all right? What happened? Where is Vlad?"

"A very good question," said Viktor coming into the cell with the other vampires. "What's the answer, Joe? Where is Vlad?"

"I don't know and that's the truth," said Joe. "But I've asked someone who does know to bring him here," he continued quickly as Valentyna floated towards Mary.

"Who have you asked?" demanded Viktor. "Why would this person help Vlad to his death?"

"He doesn't know you want to kill the young master," babbled Joe. "It's a friend of his and I've told him you and your family have gone from the castle. He thinks it's safe for Vlad to come home."

"The idiot believed you?" Valentyna asked, her mouth widening into a grin.

Joe couldn't tear his eyes from her face, mesmerised by the smile twisting her wine-red lips. Her eyes looked even redder than usual illuminated by the lantern light.

"Yes, yes, he most certainly did," said Joe, relieved to have fooled them.

"Good, then we don't need to keep either of you alive any longer. Let's get them." Valentyna signalled the twins forward, but again Viktor stopped them.

"I agree, beloved, but I think we should wait until we've dealt with Vlad. You never know when a hostage might come in handy. If all goes according to plan, they'll be dead before dawn. Leave them completely in the dark. Let the rats come out to have some fun with them."

The door clanged shut and they were left without even the candle stub in the corner. Joe held Mary tight for comfort, but thoughts of the future made him shiver.

"Do you think they're going to kill us?" Mary whispered.

"Don't worry," he said. "The villagers won't let us down."

He explained to Mary all that had been discussed at Granny Entwhistle's.

"Rexus will make Vlad's aunt tell the truth to Albert Grundig and the entire village will be on the way soon. They's sure to rescue us in time. Don't you fret about that, my dear," he finished, wishing he believed his own words.

"Oh Joe, you're such a tower of strength to me."

"Gosh, Mary, I don't know what I'd do without you," he said, glad the dark hid his blushing face. He hugged her tighter as something skittered across the floor. "Youse gotta have faith, Mary. They's on their way."

* * *

"Giddy-up, George," Rexus urged.

He'd covered the miles much faster than he'd hoped, but he still had a way to go. His thoughts wandered back to the last time he'd been to Malign village. He hoped he'd see Lisette again. More than ever he wanted his werewolf curse lifted.

Lost in his dreams of violet eyes, he was surprised to find himself almost at the edge of Dank Forest. He called George to a halt, slid from his back and tied him to a tree.

"You wait here, old boy. I'll be back soon."

He patted the donkey's head and scratched between his ears. George gave a little snort, put his head down and began munching the lush grass. Rexus brushed off his suit and strode into the village.

He passed the inn with its ominous sign of the dead vampire, and continued towards Elsabetta's house, relieved to see the street lamps were still lit. It couldn't be as late as he'd thought. He reached Elsabetta's door and knocked. It seemed like forever before he heard light footsteps approaching. The door opened and Lisette appeared. She looked so very pretty in the lamplight. Rexus opened his mouth to speak and then realised he hadn't a clue what to say.

* * *

Granny busied herself in the kitchen while she waited for Rexus to return. She sharpened her blood-letting knife on the whetstone and prepared the other ingredients she would need. She had enough fresh toads and mice, six types of fungus, marjoram, thyme, saffron, honey, wolfsbane and hemlock. All she needed now was the blood of a living hupyre.

Rexus might not like it, but his new little friend would die tonight. Why only make up a batch to cure Rexus when there would be werewolves aplenty ready to pay for a permanent cure?

Only take enough blood to treat one? No, she'd drain the hupyre completely and set herself up as *the* place to go if you had a nasty lunar curse.

Granny heard Gladys bray. How unusual, she thought. I wonder if Rexus has forgotten something and come back for it. She stood up and walked through to the front door.

"Rexus," she called. "Rexus, is that you?"

When no one answered, she went around to the back of the cottage to check on the donkey. Gladys was contentedly eating grass. Granny stared all around at the trees surrounding the clearing, but nothing moved. She went back inside.

The knife glinted in the candlelight and she smiled. The secret was to have the blade as sharp as sharp could be. That way she'd be able to keep the hupyre alive for longer. Once he was dead, the blood wouldn't be worth taking.

She gathered up her equipment and went quietly upstairs.

Chapter Nine

Elsabetta Better Watch Out

Rexus opened and closed his mouth, but no words came out.

Lisette giggled. "You look like a goldfish."

He coughed and tried again, but still he couldn't speak. Why wouldn't his stupid mouth do what it was supposed to?

"Lisette! Lisette! Who is it?"

Elsabetta's angry voice coming from inside broke the spell and the words came rushing out.

"I need to make her own up to being in cahoots with the vampires," Rexus said, "but don't worry. I won't tell her you told me – I promise."

Elsabetta appeared from behind Lisette and glared at Rexus.

"What are you doing here? Why didn't you bring my nephew as you promised? I waited up all through last night and you didn't come."

Rexus was about to come straight out and accuse Elsabetta of being hand in glove with Viktor, when he noticed Lisette's eyes go wide and her head move slightly from side to side. He couldn't ignore the pleading in her eyes and realised he might get her into trouble if he said the wrong thing.

"We got lost in the forest," he said and was immediately rewarded by Lisette's grateful smile.

"Then where is he? Why haven't you brought him to me?" Elsabetta demanded.

"Let me come inside and I'll explain."

"Very well," Elsabetta said. "Come with me!"

Rexus followed her through the hall of mirrors to the plush drawing room. Elsabetta smiled as she sat down.

"Take a seat. Lisette, what are you standing there for? Go away."

Rexus ignored the hand waving him towards one of the couches. Walking over to the drawing room door, he closed it on Lisette, locked it and slipped the key into his pocket.

"What on earth do you think you are doing?" asked Elsabetta, getting up and striding towards him.

"Saving a woman at the castle, I hope," he answered. "You told the villagers Vlad's father attacked and killed that child. Didn't you?"

Elsabetta looked shaken, but she quickly recovered.

"Yes, I did, but it was the truth. It was Count Ilya. I saw him. What else could I do, but tell everyone what I'd seen?"

Her tearful voice almost convinced Rexus, but then he spotted the sly look of triumph in her eyes.

"That's not true," he said. "You took money from Viktor and lied about what happened on the night the child died."

"Who says so? What proof do you have?" Elsabetta sneered.

"I can't tell you how I know," he said, "but it's the truth just the same. If I had brought Vlad here you would have handed him over to Viktor."

A vision of what Granny would do to Vlad later that night filled Rexus' head and a hot wave of shame surged through him. He was no better than Elsabetta. But if he could get the villagers roused quickly to save Mary, maybe he could get back in time to make sure Vlad survived Granny's knife.

"Me? In league against my own sister's husband? What utter rubbish. I've had all I'm going to take from you. Either tell me who told such lies, or get out of my house!"

Rexus had thought he could make Elsabetta tell the truth simply by saying he knew about her deal with Viktor, but everything was going wrong. He had to try and call her bluff.

"I know you took money from Viktor," he said, "and I know how much. The only way to stay out of trouble is to come with me to Ye Olde Stake House and confess everything to the landlord!"

"Are you mad?" she said, returning to her seat. "Why should I do any such thing?"

"Because they've taken a woman hostage and will kill her. But the landlord could raise the villagers and attack Castle Malign."

Elsabetta smiled at him with so much pity that Rexus wanted to disappear into the night and never be seen again.

"You stupid, deluded fool. I don't care about some woman I've never met. I don't care about my nephew. But I do care about me. I have no intention of confessing to anything, even if I *had* connived as you say I did. I don't know what you think you're up to, young man, but you'd better unlock the door and give me back my key. If you don't, it will be you the villagers will deal with, not the inhabitants of the castle. Albert may not like me, but he won't like the idea of you forcing your way in here and harassing a poor defenceless woman."

Rexus fumed at his own idiocy. Why hadn't he thought things through properly? Reluctantly he gave the key to Elsabetta, who unlocked the door.

"If you ever come back here again, I'll have you arrested. Now, get out! Lisette!" she yelled and the maid appeared. "Make sure he leaves my house and don't ever let him in again!"

They walked in silence to the front door; their footsteps on the marble sounded like a thunderous tattoo to Rexus' ears. Idiot, idiot, idiot, the beat seemed to say. Humiliated, Rexus turned his anger on Lisette as soon as they were outside.

"How come you didn't tell anyone about her and the vampires apart from me?" he hissed.

"Because I'll lose my job, that's why. I've no money and nowhere else to go. She'll throw me out if I go against her."

"Well, a woman is going to die because of you," he said, and on those unreasonable words he stalked away.

His anger carried him halfway to the inn before he realised how unfair he'd been. He forced himself to carry on walking, but his mind was screaming at him to run back and apologise. It wasn't Lisette's fault he was in such a mess. He promised himself he would put things right with her just as soon as... as soon as what? As soon as he'd allowed Granny to cast her spell? He thought of Vlad's trusting face and felt little better than ... than ... than Vlad's aunt!

There was only one thing left he could do, and that was to go to Ye Olde Stake House anyway. He knew, without Elsabetta's confession to prove his story, the chances were against Mr Grundig believing him. The landlord had made his feelings about vampires quite clear, and it wasn't going to be easy to convince him that Count Ilya had been innocent. But maybe Mr Grundig would care about Mary's fate.

He retraced his route until he arrived at the village square and sat on the bench outside the pub, planning what to say. Minutes passed, but he couldn't think of a clever way to persuade the landlord. Sighing, he stood up.

"Rexus! Rexus!"

He looked up to see Lisette sprinting across the square. She arrived gasping for breath, her cheeks like roses, and Rexus thought she had never looked prettier.

"I'll come in and tell Albert Grundig what I know," she panted. "But first, tell me about the woman who might die."

Rexus filled her in on Mary's fate and his plan to get the villagers to attack the castle.

Taking a deep breath, they entered the pub, hand in hand.

* * *

Vlad had forced himself to wait for ten minutes before silently rising off the soft mattress and creeping to the window. Trying hard not to make a sound he'd opened it just enough to climb out. The ledge was narrow and his feet only just fitted.

He was fairly certain Granny had drugged last night's chocolate. How else would he have slept for so long? The memory of falling asleep at the kitchen table had come to him just as he'd been about to down tonight's chocolate.

Had tonight's chocolate been drugged? He wasn't sure, but hadn't taken any chances. He'd poured it down the sink while Granny had been outside with Rexus. Vlad had no idea why Granny was so determined to keep him at the cottage, but he was even more determined to leave it and surrender to Viktor and Valentyna in exchange for Mary's freedom.

He clung to the window frame and looked out. The forest surrounding the cottage looked black and menacing. He realised he wasn't high enough for what he wanted to do. He'd have to climb onto the roof. Inching his body sideways, he reached out for the drainpipe next to the window. Once he had a tight grip on it, he brought one leg across. His foot searched until he felt one of the coupling joints. He put some weight on it, then some more. It held. Now for the hard part. He put all his weight on that foot and swung the other one out. He clung to the drainpipe, praying it wouldn't come away from the wall.

His fingers stretched up, seeking the next handhold. He found one in the crumbling stonework. Then he lifted his foot and felt for somewhere safe to place it. Another tiny hole in the stones, just big enough for the toe of his trainer, did the job. Inch by painful inch he climbed, until his questing fingers found the guttering under the eaves. He held on to it with both hands and dragged himself upwards. His feet scrambled for whatever toeholds they could find. A little at a time he levered himself onto the roof, until, finally, he was face down on the tiles.

Sweat poured from his face. Okay, so far, so good. All he had to do now was jump off and fly. Carefully, he turned and raised himself into a sitting position. He edged along the roof on his backside until he reached the chimney stack. Using it as a frame, he climbed to his feet and gazed out at the forest. It seemed to stretch forever.

He moved his feet to get a more secure perch on the roof and a tiny piece of slate broke. It slipped down the roof and fell to the ground. Gladys the donkey hee-hawed and Vlad froze. He waited to see if the donkey's call would bring Granny outside. Sure enough, he heard the front door open and Granny step out; light spilled from the cottage.

"Rexus? Rexus, is that you?"

Vlad waited without breathing. He heard her footsteps going round the back to where the donkey was tethered. It felt like hours before he heard her return to the front and go back inside. When the light disappeared he let out the breath he'd been holding.

Vlad clung to the chimney. He had no choice but to trust his ability to fly. He couldn't walk to the castle in time. He pulled himself up to his full height, trying to believe he could cope with anything. But a picture of him confronting Valentyna came into his mind and his chest closed in a giant wheeze. His hand went to his jeans pocket and brought out his inhaler. He sucked in deeply until he could breathe again. He had to do this. He just had to.

He was convinced that it was fear that gave him the ability to turn into a bat. The thought of jumping from the roof terrified him. So that's okay, then, he thought. If I frighten myself half to death by jumping, then I should be able to fly. Every nerve in his body jangled. He could feel his stomach sloshing and prayed he wouldn't be sick. Mary needed him, so he had no choice. Standing on tiptoe, he launched himself forward.

He dropped like a stone, straight towards Gladys. The air rushing past pulled at his skin and clothes. Just before he reached the donkey, he felt the crunch as his legs shortened. Then his arms stretched. Further and further until they became wings and he was off, soaring upwards.

From high above Granny's cottage he could see the immense Dank Forest stretching like a long black carpet in the night. As a bat, he'd cross it in less than half an hour. He might be scared of the dark, unable to breathe properly, and couldn't quite trust his sonar, but he wasn't going to let Mary down.

Once he was far enough from the cottage he grinned and screamed into the night, "Vlad the Inhaler to the rescue!"

* * *

Granny Entwhistle crept up the stairs. She tiptoed to the door and listened. Not a sound. The chocolate had done its job. With a smile of satisfaction, she opened the door and went in.

The first thing she saw was the empty bed, and then the curtains pushed to one side. Vlad had either climbed down to the ground below, or up onto the roof. But did he have enough courage for that? Below her, Gladys stood contentedly against the wall. If he had climbed down Gladys would have kicked up a huge fuss. No way would she keep quiet if her food was disturbed.

There was no other explanation, Vlad must have climbed up and flown away! Granny rushed downstairs and out of the front door as fast as her legs could take her, almost tripping on the snake as it slipped from her shoulders. She snatched it up and tied it in a knot round her neck. She had to move quickly to find Rexus and tell him Vlad had escaped. He'd have to find him and bring him back.

She looked Gladys sternly in the eye.

"I know you don't like carrying me, but this is an emergency. So, I'll have none of your nonsense," she said, mounting the bad-tempered donkey and pointing her towards Dank Forest.

"Come on, my girl. Giddy up. We've no time to waste."

* * *

Far away on a mountain top, in a nest as big as Granny Entwhistle's kitchen, a golden eagle scanned the night sky looking for supper. Its sharp eyesight picked out what appeared to be a larger than usual bat in the distance. Enormous wings unfolded and it launched itself from the nest, soaring gracefully towards its unsuspecting prey.

* * *

Vlad loved being airborne. Loved it, loved it, loved it. The feeling of weightlessness, soaring high above the forest, thrilled him. If it wasn't for what was waiting at his journey's end, he would have sung for joy. At first he'd feared his flying powers would vanish as they had before, but the longer he flew, the more confidence he had in his ability. His vision was different while he was in bat form. Tiny pinpricks of light showed him the countryside through a grey haze. Strange echo sounds beeped in his brain, but he didn't know how to unscramble them. He could see the castle turrets just a few miles away and wished he could fly faster. So intent was he on his goal that he wasn't aware of other creatures sharing the sky.

Vlad's vision remained fixed on the castle.

"Arggggggggh!"

Red hot agony sliced through his back. He twisted his head and saw the eagle's beak inches from his face. Razor-sharp talons sank deeper into his back as the claws took a firmer grip. The shock caused Vlad to lose his bat form. His shape changed and the eagle let go.

Vlad plunged downwards, flapping his arms, desperate to return to bat form, but nothing happened. He crashed through the trees, branch after branch breaking his fall, until he landed in a heap on the ground.

He opened one eye and tried to move. Every bone in his body ached, but he didn't think he'd broken anything. Cautiously he moved his arms, then both legs. One leg was cut and bleeding and his left wrist ached like crazy. His back burned and he wondered how much damage the eagle's talons had done. It felt as though he'd been sliced like a piece of meat on a butcher's slab.

He tried to stand up, but couldn't do it. He sat down again on a log. Sick with pain and fear, tears filled his eyes, but he brushed them away. He couldn't give in now. Apart from Mary needing him, the smell of his blood would attract every werewolf from miles around.

After a few minutes he felt less nauseous and forced himself to his feet. He needed to find a clearing and try to fly. But if he was too injured to fly, then he'd just have to walk. His fear of the dark made him want to curl up into a ball and hide, but he forced himself onwards through the dark and gloomy forest.

After a while he thought he heard the crunch of twigs being trampled underfoot and a feeling of being watched made him shiver.

"Who is it? Who's there?" he called out.

Chapter Ten

In a Hole, but Bearing Up

Rexus and Lisette walked into the crowded inn and Lisette gasped.

"I've never seen so many crosses in one place in all my life," she whispered, gazing at the cluttered walls. "And why is everyone staring?"

"Don't worry," Rexus said. "It's just because you've never been in here before."

Albert Grundig looked up, bushy eyebrows raised in query.

"Good evening, young sir, and what can I get you and the young lady?"

"I'm not drinking just at the moment, thank you," Rexus said. "We're here because we need your help. It's a matter of life and death."

"Well, if I can help, I'd like to, but I don't see how I can do anything in a life and death case. Are you sure you don't need a doctor?"

Rexus leant closer. "I need your help to save someone and chase the vampires out of the castle," he whispered.

Albert grinned. "Well, I'm all in favour of getting rid of vampires. Who is it that needs saving?"

Rexus took a deep breath and explained about Joe and Mary.

Albert frowned. "I don't think I know them. Are they from Malign?"

"I don't know," Rexus said. "What's that got to do with it?"

The landlord looked shocked. "It's got everything to do with whether or not people from this village will risk their lives," he said. "If they're not from here then it's not our problem."

"Do you remember Count Ilya?"

"That I do," Albert said. "I led the hunt for him. We chased him and his missus down by the river, but we got there too late. They'd already gone."

"Count Ilya didn't kill that child," said Rexus.

"Ah, but that's where you're wrong, young'un," Albert insisted. "We know he did, because his own sister-in-law saw him."

Rexus nudged Lisette.

"Elsabetta lied," she said, so quietly Rexus wasn't sure the landlord would hear her over the hub of conversation. "The new vampires paid her to say it was Count Ilya."

But he must have done because he snorted in disbelief and flicked the bar towel over his shoulder.

"Nobody would be so cruel as to get someone killed for money," he said. "That's just about the wickedest thing I've ever heard. Now, you two take yourselves off. I don't like Elsabetta Deerling, and I don't like the fact her sister married one of the vampires, but for you two to come in here and claim she would do that, well, I've never heard the like."

He moved away to talk to one of his customers further down the bar.

"What do we do now?" asked Lisette. "If Albert Grundig doesn't believe us, then neither will the other villagers. His is the most powerful voice around here."

"We'll just have to convince him."

They moved along the bar until they were in front of Albert. His scowl didn't look any better close up.

"I thought I told you two to leave," he said folding his arms.

"You did," Lisette answered, "But please, what we're saying is the truth. I heard Elsabetta talking to the vampires."

"Did you see them?" Albert asked looking down his plump nose.

"No I didn't, but ..."

"Just as well," interrupted an ancient, sucking beer through the gaps in his teeth. "You don't want to be seeing them. Nasty things, vampires. I remember ..."

"Yes, all right, Cedric. We can do without your rememberings," said Albert. He turned back to Lisette. "How do you know she was talking to vampires if you didn't see them?"

"Because she called them by their names and besides, she'd taken all sorts of precautions before they arrived."

"Garlic," said the old man. "That's the best. I remember ..."

"Shush, Cedric. What sort of precautions?" Albert asked, frowning at his customer.

"Well, she had loads of crosses under her scarf and ..."

"They're okay, crosses are, but garlic's the best," interrupted old Cedric with a grin that displayed his lack of teeth. "Did she have garlic?"

"Yes," said Lisette, "in every pocket. Oh, please, Mr Grundig, come with us to Elsabetta's house. I'm sure you could get her to tell the truth."

"He can do anything, can Albert," said Cedric. "Best bartender in Malign," he continued, nudging his empty mug towards the landlord and looking hopeful.

Albert sighed. "Any more beer and you'll fall off that stool, Cedric. If I go to Elsabetta Deerling's house and it turns out that you two are lying, I'll have you locked up. You understand? Okay, everyone," he yelled. "We're closing early tonight."

A grumble of disapproval greeted his words.

"What's up, Albert?" shouted one disgruntled customer. "I haven't finished my beer yet."

Before Albert could answer, Cedric piped up.

"We're on a vampire hunt, everyone grab some garlic," he said, staggering outside on legs that looked too bandy to carry him.

Rexus couldn't help but smile. The old man

looked like he'd just got off one of Granny's donkeys.

"Take no notice of that old fool," Albert shouted. "It isn't a vampire hunt. Not yet, at least. You remember when we all chased the vampire and his wife a little while back because Elsabetta Deerling came in here screaming she'd seen a murder? These two say we chased the wrong vampire. I'm off to Elsabetta Deerling's house to find out if she'd lied to us, or if these two are telling fibs for reasons of their own."

A murmur ran around the inn. Everyone decided to go along with Albert, Rexus and Lisette for the free entertainment. The inn emptied and all and sundry marched across the village square.

Shutters opened as they passed.

"What's going on? Where are you all off to?"

"Vampire hunting," Cedric shouted.

"Will you stop saying that for goodness sake," Albert ordered.

"Okay, Albert," said Cedric as another window opened next to him.

A man peered out. "Where're you lot going?" he asked.

"Vampire hunting," said Cedric.

People poured out to join the throng. The small crowd had grown to a very large crowd by the time they arrived at Elsabetta's front door.

Albert Grundig stepped forward and knocked. No one came, so Albert knocked again, harder this time. They heard someone shouting, but still no one opened the door. This time Albert thumped really hard and angry footsteps pounded inside. As Elsabetta opened the door, she looked over her shoulder and shouted back into the house.

"Lisette, where are you, you useless wretch? Do I have to do everything myself?"

She turned her attention to the street and took a step back in surprise at the multitude staring at her.

"Why are you hammering on my door at this hour?" she demanded. Then she spotted Lisette and Rexus standing next to Albert. "Ah, I begin to understand. What lies have those two been telling? You should know, Albert Grundig, that I don't appreciate you disturbing me because you've been listening to tales from my ex-maid and her foolish friend."

"Ex-maid?" Albert turned to Lisette. "You

didn't tell me you'd been fired. If this is just spite on your part because you lost your job ..."

"If Lisette was fired," Rexus cut in, "how come Elsabetta was calling for her to open the door?"

Albert turned back to Elsabetta. "That's a good point. If you'd thrown her out, you wouldn't expect her to be there to open the door, now would you?"

"I, I forgot. I ..."

"Well, you need to start remembering," said Albert. "We've got some questions to ask you and they've got nothing to do with whether or not you fired your maid."

* * *

A twig snapped. A flock of birds flew into the air squawking their concern to the night sky. Convinced he was being followed, Vlad struggled on, dragging his bleeding leg behind. The forest gave way to a moonlit clearing and he knew he'd have to take his chances on being seen. He moved into the open space, feeling vulnerable, as if countless eyes were watching from the darkness. He took a steadying breath and drew on thoughts of batwings and sonic sight. He'd flown twice now, so even from a standing start he should be able to take off. If he believed in himself, had faith, then surely he could …

Snap!

… another twig.

Vlad's heart thumped. It was now or never. He raised his arms to flap just as the bushes swayed and parted. Two figures burst though. It was Skinner and Bones, weapons pointing straight at him.

With a surge of adrenaline, Vlad's wings appeared and he shot upwards. His wounded leg didn't fully transform and the part-human limb dragged him down. His injured wrist meant his wing on the opposite side didn't work very well, but at least he was airborne, even if he couldn't fly in a straight line. He tried to rise higher, to put more distance between him and the bounty hunters. His damaged wing didn't give him the lift he needed, so he shot forwards, using the forest canopy as shelter. He heard the clatter as a stake rattled through the branches below.

Once out of arrow range, he forced his wings to work harder and managed to gain enough height to fly just above the tree tops. He fixed his sonic sights on the grey shape of the castle turrets. Thank goodness he hadn't got far to go. Every movement of his wings brought fresh agony.

It was no good; Vlad was in too much pain to maintain the height he needed to clear the trees. He dropped lower and flew through them, swerving left and right. Soon he found he couldn't fly at all, the branches became too dense. He'd have to walk the last part. He drifted gently to the ground, out of breath and his wounds throbbing, but pleased with himself for mastering the art of flying. Well, sort of mastering it, anyway.

But Vlad knew he had no time to waste feeling smug. Mary needed him. He limped on, trying not to think about how much he hurt. He thought only of rescuing …

"Whooooooooaaaaaaaaaa!"

Thump!

Vlad landed on his back in a deep pit with the wind knocked out of him. Fortunately, he'd landed on a pile of leaves and didn't add any more injuries to his battered body. The pit was almost pitch black apart from the middle where moonlight slanted in. He peered around while his breath returned.

It was too dark to see anything, so he thought he'd best make his way to the middle where it was a tiny bit lighter and try taking off again from there. Once he reached the patch of weak moonlight, the pit around him looked even darker, and worse, he thought he could hear movement, like a shuffling noise. What's more, a rank animal smell grew. It wasn't werewolf or deer. This was a different smell altogether.

Then he heard a grunt and a massive triangular-shaped head loomed though the darkness, jaws wide and with teeth that would have made Aunt Valentyna jealous. He realised what the pit was for – it was a bear trap.

"Noooooooo," Vlad screamed as the great beast lunged.

The world went into slow motion and then ground to a halt. The bear froze in mid-stride, reaching out for Vlad. It looked like a statue with ferocious jaws ready to snap him in two, but thankfully the animal was motionless. Its claws showed talons extended like knives. Vlad wouldn't have stood a chance if the bear could move, but why had it frozen? What was going on?

Then Vlad realised what it must be. He'd developed another vampire trait. He could control creatures with the power of his mind. Cool, he thought, his heart hammering. How about that for a nifty trick to get him out of trouble! He didn't want to be a vampire, of course he didn't, but he had to be honest, there were some parts he wouldn't want to give up in a hurry.

Vlad edged backwards, keeping his eyes on the bear. When he felt the earth wall behind him, he turned and began to climb. He used tree roots sticking out from the earth as foot and handholds and gradually pulled himself up the side of the pit. He concentrated so hard on climbing, he forgot about controlling the bear until he heard a noise. Glancing back, he saw the creature up on its hind legs, huge furry arms swiping at the air. The enraged animal lumbered towards him. Vlad scrambled up the earth bank as fast as he could. He could smell the fetid hot breath getting closer.

Whack!

A swipe of the bear's paw sent him flying into the air. He crashed into a tree just outside the pit and fell back down to earth with a crunch. His last sight was the moon disappearing from view. The night went black and he passed out.

Chapter Eleven

Timid Timms Takes a Trip

"Timms, you snivelling coward, come out this second. A grown man hiding rather than facing up to his responsibilities! What on earth do you think you look like?"

Timms had never seen Mrs Timms so angry. He peeped from behind the couch. She reached for him, but he ducked down and scurried away, reappearing behind the armchair.

"I'm not going, Mrs Timms, and that's that," he said, trying to be masterful, although his voice quavered.

"Good heavens, Timms, what do you think they're going to do? Bite you?"

"Well, um, er, they *are* vampires, dearest. That's, um, that's what they do."

"Now look here," said Mrs Timms. "This is nonsense, how many times have you been to the castle and returned safely? Not once have you been killed."

"But, dearest, it would only take once."

Mrs Timms glared, clearly not in the mood to appreciate his puny attempt at humour.

"You can't trust them. Please understand, I don't want to go," he pleaded. "This new lot are different. They're vicious and …" he stopped and shuddered. "Mrs Timms, I'm not going and that's all there is to it."

"Oh really?" she said. "We shall see about that. Until now you've only made me angry. But now I'm about to get *furious*."

Timms ducked down, curling up into a tiny ball. His fear of Valentyna had given him the strength to defy his wife, but he'd never yet seen her as mad as this. He couldn't help thinking that facing Valentyna, Viktor, the twins, even an entire town of vampires might be the easier option.

* * *

Elsabetta glowered at the hordes of commoners taking up every spare inch of her drawing room. She'd attempted to close the front door, saying she was too tired, but they'd surged forward, following Albert like rampaging sheep.

With her back pressed to the wall, she felt uncomfortably trapped. Her eyes spun as she sought for a way to turn this to her advantage. Albert stood in front of her, with Rexus on one side and Lisette on the other.

"Why are you picking on me? That girl," she said pointing to Lisette, "is a brazen, barefaced liar."

"I am not," cried Lisette. "You schemed with the vampires."

"Me?" She threw her head back and gave a false laugh. "Why would I possibly want to plot with them?"

"For the money," Lisette said bluntly. "I heard you talking about it."

"Nonsense, more lies! You're making it up."

"I did hear you. I did! You were paid to say Count Ilya attacked the child!"

The crowd noise rose on Lisette's words. They didn't like the sound of this. Had they blamed the wrong vampire?

"Rubbish," said Elsabetta. "I saw Count Ilya …"

"Where?" Albert cut in.

"Wh … what?" she stuttered.

"Where did you see it happen? It's a simple enough question. If you saw it, then you can tell us where."

"Ah, she don't like that question, do she?" said old Cedric who'd elbowed his way to the front.

The villagers murmured as one and Elsabetta squirmed.

"It was in the child's garden. I was out walking, getting a little night air …"

Rexus interrupted her. "It was not. I heard the attack and it was in the forest."

All eyes turned to Rexus.

"I knew I'd seen you before," said Albert. "As soon as you came into my inn the first time, I thought to myself, I know this young man. But when I couldn't remember where I'd seen you, I decided I must have been mistaken. But I wasn't, was I? It was you who'd insisted you'd seen the vampire and it hadn't been Count Ilya. This makes me even more suspicious now. What are you up to? Eh?"

Rexus didn't know how to answer and prayed nobody would ask why he'd been in the forest at night. Just as he was getting some very uncomfortable looks, Lisette got their attention.

"Please listen to me. I promise I heard her scheming with Viktor and Valentyna. Besides, if she's not dealing with the vampires, why is this room loaded with garlic and full of mirrors?"

Lisette lifted one of the cushions on the couch to reveal masses of garlic cloves.

"That's proof that is," said Cedric. "I remember ..."

"You don't understand," Elsabetta cried. "I was frightened of them. I had to do as they said or they'd have killed me."

"You took their money," said Albert. "You didn't have to do that."

Elsabetta's face turned ugly with rage.

"Shall I tell you why?" she snarled. "The real reason? It's because Katerina got everything. Everything! From the time she was born my parents loved her more than me. Everyone loved her. I should have been a Countess, not her. Ilya liked me before she pushed her way in. I don't care if she's my sister, I hate her."

"Well, I never did hear the like," gasped Albert. "I don't know, but I think you might be worse than the vampires."

"No, she can't be worse. There's nothing worse. I remember…"

"Not now, Cedric," Albert interrupted. "Are you telling me you let your own sister be taken away by vampires, just because you were jealous of her?"

"Not just for jealousy, whatever you might think. I was terrified. I had to do as they said. They, Valentyna and Viktor, offered me a fortune if I helped them, but they said they would kill me if I didn't. I had to help them, don't you see that?"

"No, I don't," said Albert. "You could have come to us for help. Why did you take their money?"

Elsabetta looked astonished. "It costs a fortune to keep myself in new clothes. As for the upkeep of this house, it's a nightmare."

"Let me get this straight," said Albert. "You let vampires take your own sister and then told us a pack of lies in the hope that we would attack your brother-in-law. Is that right?"

Elsabetta nodded. "I hope that half-breed

brat of his dies as well. It's not fair. Ilya loved me first. Me!"

"You're off your head," Albert said. He turned to the crowd. "Right, let's go to the castle and get rid of every vampire we find. They're evil, every last one of them. Full breeds or half-breeds, we'll wipe them out."

"Wait!" Rexus shouted. "Vlad's not evil. He's never hurt anyone."

"I don't know who to believe anymore," said Albert. "If your friend is at the castle, he'll suffer the same fate as the others. As for you," he said, turning back to Elsabetta. "You're not welcome in Malign. You'd best be gone by the time we get back."

He lifted his torch. "Okay, everyone, let's go. We need to arm ourselves. Petrus," he shouted to a man in a fireman's helmet, "get the priest to bless your truck and turn the water holy. I've got a feeling we're going to need more than just the odd bottle on this job."

The crowd surged out and dispersed to their homes, reappearing in no time at all armed with a variety of weapons. Some carried stakes; others held the mallets required to knock them in. All wore garlands of garlic pressed on them by anxious relatives. Petrus sat proudly on the front seat, holding the reins of the fire truck's four massive shire horses. Shutters opened as the army passed. Shouts of encouragement and good wishes rang out from every house.

A door opened and a man tumbled into the street. He fell flat on his face. The crowd of slayers came to a halt as the man scrambled to his feet and then dropped to his knees in anguish.

"Oh please, my dearest Mrs Timms, please reconsider."

His wife heaved through the door, like a battleship under full steam, flying her green headscarf like a pirate's flag and her purple cheeks puffed with rage.

"You'll get up to that castle and do your duty and that's final," she yelled.

Albert stepped forward and helped the trembling man to his feet.

"The castle, you say? You're going up to the castle?"

"Indeed he is," said Mrs Timms.

"No, no, no, I'm not," said Timms shaking from head to toe.

"What for?" Albert asked the angry woman.

"To view the young half-vampire's dead body and give the new owners all the assistance he can. That's his job, you see. He's a lawyer."

"I don't want to go," Timms pleaded. "Please tell her I don't have to go. I really don't think I'm cut out for this lawyering business. Perhaps I could change my job? I don't want to look at a dead body."

"But Vlad isn't dead," shouted Rexus. "He's with Granny Entwhistle over in Hungerton."

"There you are, Mrs Timms. There's no point in going to the castle after all," said Timms. "We'll go back inside, have a nice cup of tea, and then go to bed, shall we?"

"Mrs Timms can have her tea and go to bed," said Albert. "But I think you'd best come with us. We're going up to rid ourselves of all the vampires and I think it would be better if we had a lawyer with us to keep it all legal."

The crowd resumed its purposeful march. At the head was Albert. Timms brought up the rear, hiding behind the holy water wagon. He planned to make a break for it just as soon as he could. He looked up at the night sky and wondered just how many unlucky stars had shone at his birth.

* * *

When they reached the forest, Rexus looked for Lisette and found her talking to Albert. He'd hoped for a few moments alone with her, but had to say goodbye in front of the landlord.

"Aren't you coming with us?" Lisette asked with a smile and Rexus nearly gave up on Granny, her spell *and* Vlad's safety.

"I want to," he said, "but I promised my Granny I'd go straight back to the cottage. She needs me to help her tonight."

"Oh, I was hoping ..."

"Let's have a song," yelled Albert. "Come on, everyone. We'll sing the hunters' hymn."

"What were you going to say?" Rexus asked Lisette.

"Nothing," she said. "Maybe I'll see you in Malign. Goodbye."

With a wave, she turned back to the march, her voice joining in the chorus of sound.

Rexus stood until he could no longer pick her out in the crowd and then went to untie the donkey. With a sigh, he mounted and turned for home. He was more worried about Vlad than he'd thought he would be. Somehow the hupyre had made Rexus care about him. Why was that, he wondered. When the answer came to him, the truth of it almost knocked

175

him off the donkey. He'd never had a friend. He'd never had anyone to talk to apart from Granny. Vlad trusted him. A voice in Rexus' head told him to make Granny let Vlad go. A louder voice reminded him that he'd never stand a chance with Lisette while he remained a werewolf.

George's head came up and he brayed. An answering bray came through the trees. Rexus hurried George towards the sound. The bushes parted and Granny shot into view on a demented-looking Gladys.

"What are you doing here? Where's Vlad?" Rexus asked as Granny pulled Gladys to a halt.

"Gone! Escaped out of the window. Would you believe it? I knew there'd be trouble the moment that idiot said the proper word for twelve and one. And then he nearly said it again! Double the trouble. I knew it. You'll have to find him and bring him back. Hurry, it has to be tonight, or another month must pass before I can do the spell."

"Granny, I've been thinking about that …"

"Don't think," shouted Granny, scaring birds from the trees. "There's no need for thinking. Just get after the hupyre and catch him. Here," she said, handing him a small glass vial, "give him this to drink. It will enslave him. He'll do your bidding, regardless of what you tell him to do. I'll be waiting for you. I have everything ready."

Rexus reluctantly took the vial and turned George towards the castle. His head said using Vlad was wrong. He liked him. But his heart was full of violet eyes and golden hair. Stay a werewolf, or turn Vlad over to Granny? He knew he didn't really have any choice.

Chapter Twelve

Dem Bones, Dem Bones

The forest glowed yellow from the flames of hundreds of torches and everyone was upbeat and merry. Everyone, that is, apart from Mr Timms.

"Um, excuse me," he said to one of the torch bearers. "I'm thinking of changing jobs, what do you do?"

The torch bearer laughed. "I don't think you'd like my job, Mr Timms. I collect rubbish from houses and take it away to the refuse tip."

"Do you have to go to the vampires' castle?"

"No, but that's the only good thing about it. It's a smelly job. My wife says she doesn't want to come anywhere near me when I first get home."

"Really?" said Timms, his face lighting up.

"Yes, and what's more, the hours are long. I go out early in the morning and don't get back until late."

Timms grinned like a Halloween pumpkin.

"That's it," he said. "That's the perfect job for me. Would you speak to your boss and tell him I'd make a good refuse collector?"

The torch bearer edged away, but Timms, overjoyed at the thought of his new profession, hardly noticed. Long hours, the possibility that Mrs Timms would avoid him when he came home *and* a lack of vampire contact −perfect!

The army of slayers still had at least an hour's march before reaching the castle, so were not yet worried about facing the vampires. One of the men had brought along a penny whistle and was merrily tootling away while Albert's fine baritone rang out, leading the group in a marching chant.

Through the heart it's got to go.
Why they bite us we don't know.
Hammer hard and hammer fast.
You go first and I'll go last.
All the vampires will be dead,
We can sleep safe in our beds.

Dank Forest was filled with the sound of song, laughter and marching feet. Werewolves would normally attack any human crossing their land, but the marchers weren't worried. They knew the werewolves would sink back into the undergrowth at the sight of such a huge number of humans. They would be allowed to pass unmolested.

Timms had been so busy telling everyone about his new career that the words of the song hadn't sunk in. Once he listened, though, a new fear raised its head. He went in search of his friend the refuse collector, but every time he got within a few feet of him, the man moved away. Instead, he caught up with Lisette.

"Um, this song they're singing, about stakes and hammerings, I won't have to, um, you know, do it? I won't have to do any of the actual hammering, that is. I won't, will I?"

"No," said Lisette. "I'm sure Albert doesn't expect that."

"Well, I'm glad I won't have to, you know, because it's not something I'd feel comfortable doing. Did I tell you I'm giving up lawyering? I'm going to be a refuse collector."

"You have mentioned it quite a few times," she sighed, "but why do you want to change jobs?"

Timms leant forward and whispered: "No

vampires for a start. Do you think I should tell Mr Grundig that I'm giving up the law?"

"I shouldn't. He is quite determined to have you along to make sure everything is above board."

"But, um, you know, um, I'd be quite, er, quite happy to believe them, if they told me about it afterwards."

Timms looked at the burly shape of Albert Grundig striding in time with the marching chant and wondered if he could sneak home.

"Your wife seemed rather keen that you come with us," said Lisette.

Timms sighed. "Fine woman, Mrs Timms. Fine, fine woman." He sighed again. "I'm sure she'll agree I'm not cut out to be a lawyer. I think I'll make rather a good ..."

"Refuse collector," Lisette finished under her breath.

* * *

High above the forest the twins searched for movement. Boris saw the lights through the trees and dropped lower to investigate, taking care not to get too close. He hovered over the treetops and listened to the words of the song. When he realised what they were singing, he rushed back to the castle.

"Mama! Mama! MAMA!" he screamed as he flew in through the window. "People, humans, lots of them, all coming this way. It looks like an uprising. How exciting, I've never seen one before. They have st ... sta ... long pieces of wood and ha ... ham ... the other word we never say – and, and, and they're singing about ki ... ki ... killing all the vam ... vampires."

"Enough!" Valentyna cried. "Where is Gretchen?"

"I don't know," said Boris. "She was flying behind me. I flew back so fast I expect she couldn't keep up."

"An uprising isn't always a good thing, Boris. Although it can be very exciting – as long as we win, of course. How far away are they, and did they have your snivelling cousin with them?"

"I couldn't see Vlad; maybe they've already killed him. They'll be here in less than half an hour, I think," Boris answered. "Is there going to be a war? Shall we kill lots of them? Can I have some as my very own prisoners? Can I? Can I?"

Valentyna smiled and patted him on the head.

"Boris, you're simply too, too, beautiful, my son. Of course you may take as many prisoners as you wish, but only when your beloved papa says so. We aristocrats have to keep up standards, you know. The rabble expect it of us."

Suddenly there was a loud screeching sound and Gretchen came flying through the window, far too fast to land gracefully.

"Aaaaaaaaaaaaahhhhhhhhhhgggggghh." She slid along the floor and landed in a heap at Valentyna's feet.

"Mama, oh Mama," she panted. "I hovered above them and heard their plan. They're singing some stupid song about driving st … sta … sta … *things* and ha … ham … But they won't win, will they?"

"My poor child," Valentyna soothed. "They can't win. The slayers can't enter the castle unless someone lets them in. They'll rant and rave, and then they'll get bored. They'll be gone before morning. Did you see the wheezy little hupyre with them?"

Gretchen shook her head.

"Then you must watch for him. Unless, of course," she said with a smile, showing her vicious incisors, "the hopeless little rat wanders into the path of the slayers. In the meantime, I'm going to the library to tell your father what is happening. Ever since he discovered the teachings of Confusingus I can't get him to keep his feet on the floor."

* * *

At that precise moment, Vlad was drifting in and out of consciousness. His head thumped and his senses swam. He tried to get up, but the dizziness made him feel like throwing up and he had to lie down again. He kept thinking he could hear singing, but knew he must be imagining it. No way would there be a choir in the forest. Still, it seemed like a pleasant tune, even if it wasn't real. Da, da, da-da, da, da, da. He hummed along. Strange, the singing seemed to be getting louder. He tried again to get to his feet by feeling his way up the trunk of a tree. The dizziness worsened, he swayed from side to side and lost his balance.

He grabbed at the trunk, but missed it and knocked himself out on a thick branch.

When he next came round, the forest was blacker than ever. His head ached, his wrist, back and leg were on fire. He couldn't bear to move. Everywhere hurt.

Then he heard voices.

"Come on, hurry up, Bones. Kill him. You know I can't stand vampires."

"I gotta do it right. It's not like your lot. Werewolves is easy. A quick shot with a silver bullet and it's all over. You've got it made, you have. Bang and they's dead, but vampires is different. You gotta consign vampires."

"What?"

"Consign 'em. To the pits of hell. You gotta do it right. It's tradition. I consign thee, foul fiend …"

Vlad forced his head in the direction of the voices.

"He moved! Quick, Bones, never mind all that rubbish. He moved."

"I consign thee …"

Vlad tried to get up, but his body refused.

"Bones! Faster, man! He's gonna get us."

"Iconsigntheefoulfiendtothepitsofhell."

"Wait!" Vlad shouted.

As before, time slowed and then stopped. Bones stood with hands raised. Skinner was frozen in place behind a tree. Vlad concentrated hard. If he could hold them long enough he might be able to escape before the spell wore off. He edged away from the tree and pain such as he had never known shot through him.

Instantly, Vlad's hold over the two men faltered. Bones reached for his bow. As waves of nausea attacked Vlad, he struggled to overcome his agony. Bones had fixed a stake into his bow before Vlad was able to pull himself together.

"Stop!" he yelled and the tableau froze. "I don't know if you can hear me, but I want to offer you a deal. If you let me live, I'll entice the vampires out of the castle for you. Kill me and you'll lose any chance of getting at my aunt and uncle."

Sweat dripped from his face as he felt the power weakening. He couldn't hold them any longer. He shut his eyes and waited for the thin stake to strike. Nothing happened, so he risked a look. Bones still had the weapon aimed at him.

"What do you reckon, Skinner? I'd love to have a crack at them vamps from the castle."

Skinner peered from behind the tree. "You can't trust him. He tried to bite me a couple of nights ago."

"That's because you were going to shoot my friend," Vlad said.

Skinner grinned. "I'll tell you what you should do, Bones. Get him to entice the castle vamps out and make him give up his werewolf buddy to me."

Vlad looked down so that they wouldn't see the anger in his eyes. Give up Rexus? As if he would. Once he was sure he had his features under control, he looked up again.

"That might be trickier," he said. "I don't know where Rexus is at the moment, but I can lead you to him once the castle vampires are gone. Does that sound like a good deal?"

"You're an odd sort of vampire, ain't ya?" Bones said, with the stake still aimed squarely at Vlad's heart. "Fair hair, blue eyes and now I hear you're friends with a werewolf. What sort of vamp are you?"

"I'm not a vampire," Vlad said. "I'm a hupyre."

"Give over. They don't exist except in fairy tales," Skinner snorted. "Have you ever met one in all your travels, Bones?"

"I never did, not even in the depths of the forest. I'm just thinking this hupyre might be worth more to me than all the castle vamps put together. I bet someone would pay a small fortune to have a hupyre's head mounted over their fireplace. I don't think I want your offer, thanking you kindly, young hupyre, but I surely do want your head once I've chopped it off. Nothing personal, you understand."

Anger surged through Vlad as Bones drew back the string on his bow. He wasn't going to allow this *human* to hurt him. He rolled over as the sharp point of the stake swept towards his heart, missing him by inches. As Bones fumbled to load another piece of wood into his bow, Vlad forced himself upright and spread his arms.

He hungered for blood and the humans were right there. He felt his fangs getting longer. It would be so easy. All he had to do was grab … No! What was he thinking? That wasn't what he wanted to do. But he did. He *needed* to drink. No, no. He put his hands to his head and screamed as his hands passed straight through. He was disappearing!

"He's getting away, Bones. Do something."

A terrible chill ran through Vlad as his body

evaporated. Slowly he turned into a cloud of dark mist, and drifted away from danger.

The bear pit was a gaping hole to his right. He could hear the bear's claws tearing at the earth and tree roots as it attempted to climb out. He could hear the bounty hunters shouting.

But as he swirled about them, the biggest noise was going on inside his head. Part of him said leave now, you need to save Mary, but another voice, getting louder and stronger, said don't leave, stay and feed. He hungered for blood and it was here for the taking.

Chapter Twelve (plus one)

Short, Dark and Misty

Rexus pushed George to go as fast as he could and caught up with the tail end of the marching villagers. He saw the lawyer trudging alongside the water truck and smiled as he trotted past. He'd never seen anyone look so miserable while singing a cheerful song.

He scanned the crowd for Lisette, spotting her golden hair in the middle of a pack of singers. Slipping off the donkey, Rexus made his way over to her side, leading George by the rein.

As she saw him, she blushed a deep rose. Surely that must mean she liked him? Rexus prayed that was the case.

"I thought you had to do something for your Granny," she said. "You must have finished very quickly."

"It's a long story. I'll tell you about it one day," he said. "Vlad escaped, I mean, flew away and Granny thinks he's in the castle."

"And you've come to rescue him?" As she said the words, she took Rexus' hand and squeezed it. "You're so brave."

No, I'm not, he thought. I'm a … I'm a … I don't know what I am, but whatever it is, I hope Lisette never finds out.

Out loud, he said, "I'm going to see if I can find him, but if he is in the castle I don't know if I'll be able to get in."

She smiled. "I'm sure you'll manage. I'm so glad you've come back. I heard someone say there were werewolves near here. I hate werewolves. I'm even more scared of them than vampires. At least with vampires it's only one bite and that's it." She lowered her voice. "Werewolves are disgusting creatures. You can smell their stench for miles and they actually eat their victims. Can you imagine that?"

"No," said Rexus weakly, "I can't. I can't imagine that at all."

Her words hit him like a sledgehammer and his hand reached into his pocket to reassure himself the vial Granny had given him was safe. After tonight there'd be no chance of her finding out that he was one of the creatures she most feared.

As the vampire slayers marched from the cover of Dank Forest, the cheerful and rousing chant began to falter. Earlier, being brave had been easy, but the sight of Castle Malign looming ahead of them choked their merriment. Vast, dark and brooding, the castle looked impossible to penetrate. The drawbridge was down, but the enormous gates were securely closed.

Albert continued his purposeful stride and the others, none of whom wanted to appear a coward, felt obliged to keep up with him. Apart from Timms, who felt safer hiding behind the holy water truck.

Rexus joined Albert at the front. Although his stomach felt as if it was full of squirming caterpillars, he knew it didn't pay to show fear to vampires. Everyone had garlic and Petrus was busy filling empty containers of all shapes and sizes with holy water.

Albert led his army to the drawbridge and called out to the vampires looking down from the balcony.

"Excuse me, sir, but we need to have a word

with you about an incident that took place a little while ago."

"How entertaining," Viktor called down. "So you haven't come to pay us a social call? You're most welcome to join us for a little snack."

"How amusing you are, my beloved," said Valentyna. "Oh look! They have a cart. We could have several rolled in – meals on wheels."

"Sir!" shouted Albert, who believed in being polite, even when dealing with vampires. "I'd like to ask you a question, if you don't mind. Was it you who flew away with a child from our village?"

Viktor laughed. "So many meals, how am I to remember one in particular?"

Rexus stepped forward and pointed at Viktor. "That's the one I saw in the forest," he said.

"Of course it was," sneered Viktor. "My pathetic brother had lost his taste for blood. He was a disgrace to our noble name. My charming wife pointed out how unfair it was that he should squander my inheritance."

"I knew it," shouted Rexus. "I knew it wasn't Count Ilya."

"Well, it certainly seems he wasn't guilty on *that* occasion," Albert said, turning to his army. "Right lads, we're going to have to break in. We need to cut down a tree to use as a battering ram."

Rexus edged his way back to Lisette.

"I'm going to see if I can get in around the side of the castle and find Vlad if he's in there."

"Rexus, I …" Lisette's rose-tinted blush burned bright red in the torchlight. "I … be careful and come back safely. Okay?"

He didn't want her to know how scared he really was, so he just smiled and nodded.

"Don't worry, Lisette," he said, wrapping his scarf securely round his neck. "I've got lots of protection. I'll be fine."

* * *

Floating dreamily around the treetops, a swirling mist as dark as the night, Vlad tried to block the voices of Skinner and Bones, forcing himself to think only of saving Mary. He didn't want to drink their blood. Of course he didn't. He hated the taste of it. No, he didn't hate it. He loved its metallic tang. He wanted to drink.

He needed to feed. His mind seemed to be fragmented into thousands of tiny particles, all arguing for something different. He focussed hard on the non-vampire parts, forcing them to come together and fight against sucking the bounty hunters dry. Eventually, his desire for blood faded and he allowed himself to drift away until he could no longer hear the men; it was time to reform his body.

Vlad concentrated and his misty form swirled down to a clearing in the forest.

He had no idea how to change back again. He didn't even understand how he'd become dark mist in the first place. Then a terrible thought struck him. Maybe this was it. This was how he would stay for the rest of his life. A lonesome black cloud drifting through the forest - forever.

He thought about his life before Valentyna and the others arrived to ruin it. He'd had a nice home, good parents, people who loved him, Mary. Mary! He had to save her. He concentrated on being solid. Nothing happened. Maybe he had to visualise himself as human. He tried again. Still nothing. Okay, what does a body need that mist doesn't? Food, that's what. Peaches worked for him when he ate the honey, maybe thinking about peaches would work again now.

He visualised the texture of the succulent flesh, the sugary, sweet taste of the juice, the feel of the soft downy skin ... With a rush, as if he was being sucked down a plughole, millions of atoms spun into a spiralling whirlpool. He felt his body being dragged inwards to form a solid core. Instead of seeing through thousands of eyes, his vision settled back to only two. Slowly, slowly, he became solid.

He. Loved. Peaches.

The last few atoms rearranged themselves with a judder, Vlad slumped to the ground. All the pain he'd felt before returned now that he had a body once again. He hurt so much he wanted to stay right here in the forest and go to sleep. But he couldn't, Mary needed him. He dragged himself upright and tried to turn into a bat, but nothing happened. He was too injured; he'd have to walk. Sighing, he began the long slog to the castle.

After what felt like an eternity had passed, he finally approached the edge of Dank Forest. He could hear voices, so he crept from tree to tree until he was close enough to see Castle Malign. Vlad froze. Hundreds of people were brandishing stakes and hammers. Flaming torches lit up the front of the castle. He could see his aunt and uncle on the balcony overlooking the drawbridge, their grinning faces flickering yellow in the torchlight. Keeping to the shadows, he searched for Rexus, but he was nowhere to be seen.

How could he give himself up in exchange for Mary with all these vampire slayers between him and the castle gates? He'd never make it as far as the drawbridge before one of them spotted him. He'd have to sneak in through the secret tunnels.

He was about to creep towards some rocks that hid one of the entrances, when he spotted Boris swooping overhead. His cousin hovered, scanning the edge of the forest. Vlad's heart sounded like a frenzied drum; he was sure Boris would hear it. The thought of having to tackle his ferocious cousin made him dizzy. His chest tightened. Just when he thought he would pass out from the effort of controlling his breathing, Boris flew off.

A ragged wheeze forced its way out. Vlad dragged out his inhaler and sucked. When he could breathe again he took deep gulps of cold fresh air, filling his lungs. Phew! That was too close, Vlad thought. Right, no time to lose, he had to get to the tunnels before Boris returned.

He crouched down and crept across the clearing to the rocks hiding the entrance. He paused for breath and peered over the top; surely no one had spotted him? Satisfied, he ducked down and entered the dark passageway. Trying to be as quiet as he could, he crept along the murky passages. Cobwebs clung to him. Little spiders tickled over his face and scuttled down his back. He took a step and his foot landed on something squishy. It squealed. He lifted his foot and a giant rat ran off. Vlad suffocated a scream. If only he could turn back, but thoughts of Mary in trouble kept him going. Eventually the tunnel came to an end and he was in the dungeon area beneath the castle.

At least now he was where he needed to be. All he had to do was go up through the castle, get to the balcony and give himself up. He would insist that Viktor let Mary go. He'd refuse to translate the rhyme unless they did. Once the lawyer told him the verse and he'd told Viktor the secret of solving it, he'd be killed, he knew that. He just hoped they would kill him quickly and not find ways to make his death last for days. Trying to be brave, he forced himself onwards down the final gloomy corridor.

He came to the end, and was about to mount the spiral stairs leading up to the castle, when he heard voices. He stepped back and hid behind one of the thick stone columns that supported the floor above. Hardly daring to breathe, he listened. The voices came from the dungeon cell on the other side of the column and Vlad was sure he recognised them. It was Mary and Joe.

He tiptoed around and reached for the key hanging outside the cell. Lifting it down, he inserted it into the lock. The door opened with a creak and he stepped into the dungeon. Joe leapt in front of Mary.

"You'll have to kill me first," he yelled.

"Joe!" said Vlad. "Joe, it's me. I've come to save you."

"Oh mercy, me," gasped Mary. "It's my little Vlad."

She rushed forward and drew him to her in a massive hug and he had to bite his lip not to cry out in pain.

"Did Rexus bring help?" asked Joe.

"Yes, there's a huge crowd outside the castle

gates. I think Rexus must be in there with them. If we sneak out the way I came in, you'll be safe with the villagers."

The three crept silently along the tunnel to the entrance. Vlad went first, his heart filled with pride. He'd saved Mary all on his own. It almost stopped his body from hurting. Almost, but not quite. He limped on his damaged leg. His wrist and head ached, and his back, where the eagle's talons had sliced into him, was burning like crazy. But, *he'd* saved Mary *and* Joe.

They were nearing the end of the tunnel when Vlad saw a shadow swoop across the entrance. He stepped back, stopping Joe and Mary from going any further, and swallowed hard to prevent himself from being sick. He'd thought he'd saved Mary and Joe, but now they were all trapped. Boris settled on a rock outside and it looked as though he intended to be there for some time.

Vlad signalled to Mary and Joe to stand still and not make a sound. Every so often he peered around the bend in the tunnel to see if Boris had left. There were other tunnels, but he couldn't take the chance on going back through the underground network. They might run into another of his relatives.

Finally, their patience was rewarded. Boris turned his head and stared into the distance. He appeared to be listening for something. Then he switched to bat form and took off. Vlad signalled to the Greenings to come forward and grabbed Joe's arm.

"You must run with Mary to the trees. Stay in the shadows until you can join the crowds at the front of the castle."

"But what about you, master Vlad? Aren't you coming with us?"

Vlad shivered, but stood his ground.

"No, I've been thinking. The villagers need to get in, but they won't be able to unless I help them. I'll have to go and open the gates. You and Mary must go. Quickly now, before Boris comes back," he said, trying to sound brave, but his voice wobbled.

"Joe, you'd best go with him …" Mary began.

Vlad shook his head. "No. I'll be able to sneak around and hide much easier if I'm on my own. Besides, if they catch you, they'll …"

He broke off as a terrible scream sounded.

"That sounds as though Boris has caught someone. Run now while he's busy. Please, Joe, take Mary."

"Okay, master Vlad, but you be careful," Joe said grabbing Mary's arm.

Vlad waited until he knew Joe and Mary had reached the safety of the trees. He'd never felt so alone, or so scared. It was all he could do to stop himself from running after them. But he had a duty to the people of Malign village. They didn't deserve to have Viktor and Valentyna preying on them. He took a deep breath to bolster his courage and headed back down the tunnel.

* * *

On the balcony above the castle's entrance the vampires laughed at the army's attempts to batter the gates.

Viktor smiled at Valentyna. "You were right, my darkest daymare, this is going to be such wonderful fun. With so many witnesses to our power, the villagers will learn that it's safer not to meddle in vampire affairs. Did I tell you some of the words of the great Confusingus? Confusingus, he say, 'vampires suck'. Isn't that clever?" he said roaring with laughter.

"Viktor, are you feeling all right? You don't

think you're taking this meditation thing too seriously? I think we need to decide how many we should kill to teach them a lesson. One each tonight and a couple to snack on later?" Valentyna suggested.

Gretchen laughed. "Mama, don't forget you promised Boris and me some toys."

"Quite right, my little dark angel, let's make it a round dozen, shall we?"

Her gaze swept the scene in front of the castle. Campfires and torches illuminated a sea of pitched tents and the smell of vegetables cooking assaulted her sensitive nostrils.

"What do you think you'll achieve by camping out like this, you common wretches?" she shouted. "We are the elite. The upper crust. You can't possibly hurt us. As soon as that wretched Timms arrives, the castle will be ours. I give you fair warning, I won't have vile commoners such as you soiling my doorstep."

Albert shouted back. "Madam, Timms is here, but he says you need to produce proof that your nephew is dead."

"Where is he?" Valentyna scowled. "Why hasn't the little twerp come forward? My husband sent for him hours ago."

Timms crouched down and tried to crawl

under the water truck, but at the mention of his name, several men dragged him out and pushed him forward. Sighing, he gave up fighting his bad luck and went to stand next to Albert.

"Er, hello, sir, ma'am," he called. "You, um, sent for me."

"There you are, at last," Valentyna shouted. "Tell this stinking rabble to go home. The castle and grounds are ours and they're trespassing."

"I'm afraid, I'm, um, afraid, I can't do that, because they're not. They're not yours, that is, the grounds … or the castle, you see they belong to young Vladimir, unless, um, you can show me proof that he's, you know, dead."

Albert clapped Timms on the shoulder and he almost fell flat on his face.

"Well done, Timms, that told 'em." He turned back to the vampires. "You lot had better watch out. We will find a way to break in, even if it takes us days."

"You'll never manage it," sneered Valentyna. "You should all pack up and go home."

"We're not going anywhere." Albert shouted back. "We've got stakes and hammers and we're ready to use them."

"And garlic, we've got that, too," shouted

old Cedric, adding his mite to the threat. "Vampires don't like garlic. I remember …"

"Take that revolting old man away," Viktor shouted. "We don't like to bite skin as leathery as that. I can see I shall have to give you some entertainment." He turned to Valentyna. "My darkest one, go and fetch the male Greening from the dungeon. I'm sure these idiots will move away rather than watch us have our evening meal."

"What about the female Greening?" asked Valentyna. "Shall I bring her as well?"

"No, let's save her for when the hupyre arrives. We can feast on her in front of him."

"Did you hear that, you rabble?" Viktor shouted down as Valentyna floated away. "If you stay, you'll see one of your friends being part of our feast. Confusingus, he say, vampires suck."

"Papa, you've already said that once," Gretchen said.

"I know, but I like saying it," Viktor said. "I shall meditate until food arrives." He took up his elevated cross-legged position and ommed to himself.

Valentyna's rapid return brought him rapidly crashing down to earth.

"They've gone," she hissed. "I don't know how they did it, or where they are now, but the Greenings have escaped."

"What?" Viktor bellowed. "They must still be in the castle somewhere. Only the family knows the way out through the tunnels."

"Ah, but of course!" smiled Valentyna. "*Vlad* must have freed them. They can't get out because Boris is guarding the entrances. We have that revolting hupyre and his protectors exactly where we want them."

Chapter Fourteen

One in the Eye for Boris

Rexus explored the outer walls of the castle looking for a place to climb. He could swim across the moat easily enough, but the walls were sheer and he couldn't see any possible toeholds. He carried on searching without success, until he came to an enormous pile of rocks on the edge of the moat and noticed a tiny sliver of light shining from behind them. Intrigued, he climbed to the top, pulled some of the smaller rocks to one side, and found a small opening. He heaved a few of the larger rocks away to reveal a narrow tunnel heading down under the moat – a secret entrance!

Suddenly, there was a massive whooshing sound and Boris swooped down in front of him. The shock made Rexus jolt backwards and he tumbled to the bottom of the rock pile followed by the snarling vampire. Long pointed fangs headed straight for his throat. Rexus pulled his scarf tighter around his neck and the vampire bit deep into the woolly folds.

Boris yelped and staggered backwards, covering his mouth with his hand. Thick green foam poured from between his fingers.

"What's wrong? Don't you like the taste of garlic?" asked Rexus unfolding his scarf to reveal a necklace of fat, juicy garlic cloves.

Rexus took a step forwards, pretending concern. Boris howled and backed away, still trying to spit out the garlic remains.

"I'm sorry," Rexus taunted. "Does it hurt? Well, I hope *this* does, as well," he said, he uncorked a bottle and threw holy water into Boris' face.

Boris covered his eyes and screamed, clutching at his steaming face, then he shot into the air like an out of control firework rocket, trailing steam behind him.

Rexus was about to investigate the source of the light he'd spotted before Boris dropped in, when he spotted movement in the trees opposite. To his amazement, Joe and a woman left the cover of the trees and ran towards the front of the castle. If they were free, then Vlad must be as well. Grinning fit to bust, he ran to catch up with the Greenings.

* * *

The scream tore through the night air. A howl of such anguish that everyone stopped to listen. The vampires were ecstatic. They never tired of the sound of someone in pain.

Valentyna shivered. "Someone is hurt," she purred. "I hope whoever it is suffers for a long, long time."

The screaming came closer. The pain in the victim's voice sounded like a concerto. The vampires stood enthralled by the beautiful melody. Viktor ommed in tune with his inner vampire. But something wasn't quite right.

"Why are the revolting peasants cheering?" asked Valentyna.

"Look," screeched Gretchen. "Isn't that Boris?"

She pointed to a bat flying in spirals. It went up, looped-the-loop, fell a few metres, then shot up again, looping-the-loop once more, before spiralling totally out of control.

To Valentyna's fury, an even louder cheer went up.

"Hurray, one of the vampires is hurt."

Soon everyone was looking up at the squealing, spinning bat.

"Mama, it is Boris, it really is," crowed Gretchen. "May I go and finish him off? Oh, please say yes. He looks as though he'll die quickly if I go straight for the kill."

"Certainly not! How many times do you have to be told vampires don't kill other vampires? Go and help him. And tell him to stop screaming like a human. It's embarrassing."

"I don't see why I can't kill him," Gretchen sulked. "What's the point of having a brother?" she muttered as she flew to Boris' side and guided him to the balcony.

He was still howling when he landed and changed into his human form. An angry red stain dotted with white blisters covered one half of his face and one eye was swollen and closed.

"Go with Gretchen to the kitchen and put some raw meat on your face. And stop your bleedin' snivelling. You're giving me a headache," said Valentyna.

She'd been looking forward to a feast and

now hunger was making her irritable. She waited until the twins left the balcony, and then focussed her attention on Viktor who was dealing with his stress by tuning in to his inner vampire. She didn't feel quite as loving towards her death-mate as she usually did. She wasn't at all happy with the way things had turned out. In fact, she felt just a teensy-weensy bit *annoyed* with Viktor.

"Shall I go and look for the hupyre and his friends?" she asked, trying hard not to snarl.

Viktor dropped to the ground.

"What a good idea, my heartless one," he said. "I'll come with you. I want to stop off at the library to see what Confusingus has to say when plans go awry."

* * *

Vlad wished someone was there to help him. He knew where the key to the gates was kept, but had no idea how to get to it without being seen. The key room was in full sight of the balcony!

He inched along the corridors, staying against the walls as much as possible, but there were times when he had to cross vast shadowy rooms. Each time he did so, he felt exposed, expecting one of his family to appear. His entire body throbbed, he was in agony. He kept his inhaler close to his face, terrified he'd give himself away by wheezing. If only he were older and braver. More than anything, he wished someone else could let the villagers into the castle.

Nearing the Great Hall, he heard voices and ducked behind a carved chest. His breathing was so loud and ragged he was sure he'd be heard. The voices grew louder.

"Why didn't you die?"

"Because you don't die from that stuff, it just burns. Why don't you shut up?"

"Why should I? I wish you had died, then I could be an only child."

There was an almighty crash and Boris' curses filled the air. Gretchen's pretty voice tinkled with laughter as something metal clanked and clattered across the stone floor.

"You did that on purpose, Gretchen. You let me walk into that stupid suit of armour. I hate you."

"Not as much as I hate you. Anyway, if you want to walk about with your eyes covered in raw meat, why should I care if you fall over things?"

"I'll kill you one day."

"Not if I kill you first …"

Vlad waited until he could no longer hear the twins arguing and then crept out from behind the chest. The suit of armour that used to stand at the foot of the great marble staircase was scattered in pieces across the flagstones. He'd never thought he'd be pleased that Boris and Gretchen were so vicious, but if they hadn't been so hateful to each other, they'd have heard him wheezing.

He tried to calm his chest, but it was so difficult. The only thing that would help his asthma was for him to get out of the castle as soon as possible.

Vlad forced himself to continue his journey through the castle. Never had his home seemed so vast. For the first time he was aware of how many rooms there were. He decided that if he survived, although that didn't seem very likely, he would invite some friends to come and share the castle with him. Funny, it had never seemed too big when his mum and dad were there, but now it seemed to be enormous.

The next door brought him into the grand

213

dining room. A ridiculously long table ran down the middle with fifty chairs around it. That made Vlad smile. He knew there were fifty because he'd learned to count in this room. Then his smile quivered and he felt a tear forming and that awful tight feeling in his chest. Stop it, he thought and walked along running his hand over the chair backs, counting them in his head. One, two, three …

Then he froze. More voices. He spun, frantically looking for a hiding place and spotted the little couch behind the door. He ran for cover and crouched down behind it just as Valentyna and Viktor burst into the room.

"But, but, but, my angel of death," Viktor argued. "How was I to know he would escape? Besides, it was you who told the children they could play with him. If you hadn't, Timms would have told Vlad the rhyme and we could have thrown him to the werewolves. Our troubles would have been over."

"But they ain't, is they?" hissed Valentyna. "We 'ave a bleedin' rabble at the gates, our prisoners have escaped, Boris is 'urt and Ilya's brat is still runnin' round loose somewhere." Vlad heard a deep intake of breath. "I must speak nicely. I'm one of the upper crust. I'm

214

one of the upper crust. I'm one of the upper crust."

"Valentyna, you're repeating yourself."

"I know that, Viktor. I'm just reminding myself why I married you in the first place. Your nephew has made you look stupid, but not for much longer. I'm *not* going to let him beat *me*. You go up to the bed chambers and search. I'll take the dungeons. Between us we'll find him. When we do, I'm going to open his jugular. I may not be allowed to drink him, but I can still have the pleasure of watching him die, one drop of blood at a time."

Vlad waited until he was sure they'd gone before letting go of his breath. He'd held it in from the second he'd heard their voices and was almost suffocating. He dragged air into his tortured lungs, feeling as though he might as well sound the gong standing in the corner, because his wheezing rattled like thunder.

He limped from the dining room to the main hallway and, keeping to the walls, crept towards the front door, all the time listening for his horrid family. Finally, he reached the massive oak door. Heart in his mouth, he cautiously opened it. Thankfully no squeaking hinges gave his presence away. But when he looked out, he realised he'd have to cross the open area between the main building and the outer castle walls. The key hung in a small room next to the gates.

He stepped into the shadows and peered up at the balcony where the vampires had been earlier. He knew where Viktor and Valentyna were, but not his cousins. He breathed a sigh of relief – the balcony was empty. Running across the open space, he reached the safety of the key room. He took the key from its hook and edged his way to the big metal gates.

He almost wept; the lock was too high for him to reach. Then he realised the gates were far too heavy for him to open, even if he could get to the lock. He'd have to go all the way back through the castle, down to the dungeon area, along the tunnels, and then take the key to the villagers. He remembered quite clearly where Valentyna said she was going to search – the dungeons. Fear, such as he'd never before experienced, flooded his body and he trembled. He couldn't do it. He was too young, too weak from his injuries, too small to be a hero, and far too scared. Holding the key as if it were somehow the answer to all his prayers,

Vlad sank to his knees in despair. He simply couldn't do any more.

But then he looked up at the solid metal the gates and realised there might be another way to get the key out. The gates were crisscrossed with bars to strengthen them. Taking the deepest breath he could, he started to climb. He puffed and wheezed and was almost at the top when he heard Valentyna screeching.

"There's the bleedin' hupyre freak. Get 'im!"

He looked back and saw his cousins swooping towards him. He quickly scrambled up the last few rungs and threw one leg over the top of the gates. Boris' claws reached out, but Gretchen shoved her brother out of the way.

Veering from side to side to avoid first one twin, then the other, Vlad lost his grip and went tumbling over, landing with a thud on the drawbridge.

Chapter Fifteen

Vampires All at Sea

Rexus ran after the Greenings, calling out for them to stop, but it was no use. With no prospect of entering the castle immediately, the potential slayers were having a party and the noise of all the singing and merriment drowned out his shouts. He pushed his way through the crowd, looking in all directions and eventually found the Greenings.

"I'm so glad to see you two," Rexus said, "but where's Vlad?"

"Are you the one my Joe told me about?" cried Mary. "Vlad's gone back into the castle; you've got to help him. He freed us, dear brave boy that he is, but then he went to open the gates. He's going to die, I know it. My poor master Vlad is going to die."

"*Vlad* freed you?" asked Rexus. "Well, well, well. Fancy that. I didn't think he had it in him. How did you two get out?"

"Master Vlad led us through miles of tunnels," Joe said. "But it's no good asking which way we came. We took all sorts of twists and turns before we reached the entrance."

Mary's tears gleamed in the torchlight and trickled down her cheeks.

"Are you saying you can't get in to help my little one? They'll kill him," she cried, collapsing into Joe's arms.

Rexus patted Mary on the back. "Don't worry," he said. "I'll think of something."

But he knew his words were just that – words. There was nothing he could do to help Vlad.

* * *

"We 'ad 'im in our grasp and you let 'im get away," Valentyna raged, not caring a jot that her posh accent had disappeared completely. She was so angry with her children, her husband, Vlad and the entire world that she wanted to rip everyone to shreds – and if she dropped some aitches while she was doing it, too bad. She wasn't very impressed with her upper class husband just at the moment.

"It was *her* fault. She did it on purpose," Boris wailed.

"Huh," said Gretchen. "If I'd been doing anything on purpose, I'd have thrown more of that ho … ho … wa … wa … burning stuff over you."

"You can't even say it, so how could you throw it?"

"Shut up," Valentyna screamed. "Shaddup, shaddup, shaddup! I'm losing me bleedin' marbles and all you two can do is argue."

"Why are you shouting at our children, Valentyna?" asked Viktor. "It's not their fault your grand scheme to take over my brother's castle went wrong. Besides, if you could control your temper for just a few moments I would be able to hear myself think. I have another idea."

"Oh really? And will this one be any better than the others? What are we going to do? Omm Vlad back over the gates?"

"Confusingus, he say, 'sarcasm is the refuge of the lower classes' so do be careful, beloved. Your origins are showing. No, my idea is to offer a reward to the villagers. If they turn

Vlad over to us we'll give them lots of money. Look at Katerina's sister; she'll do anything for money. It's a human thing, I read about it in the collected works of Confusingus."

Valentyna thought for a moment. She hadn't liked that dig about her origins. Viktor would pay dearly for that later.

"It *might* work," she agreed through clenched teeth.

"I'm sure it will," Viktor beamed. "I'll give them the money only after we have Vlad in our hands."

"Come, children," said Valentyna. "Your dear papa is going to *try* to get it right this time."

They flew to the balcony, and Viktor shouted for the leader of the rabble to come forward.

Albert Grundig strode to the front.

"Look down there on the drawbridge," Viktor said. "You want a vampire to kill, there's one there for you. Bring me his dead body and you can have ten thousand rupeks."

Vlad's head spun. Viktor's yelling brought him round. He blinked at the flickering torchlight and recognised the man from the pub. Every bone in his body ached. He forced himself to his feet and leaned against the metal gates.

Albert Grundig stood at the end of the drawbridge surrounded by Vlad's friends.

"You can't kill him," said Mary. "He saved our lives."

"He hasn't done anything wrong," said Rexus.

"'taint right," Joe said. "They's nasty folk you're dealing with. You listen to my Mary. Master Vlad is a hero."

The crowd behind Albert were growing restless. Some were shouting, some mumbling, but Vlad heard the word kill over and over again.

Albert shouted above the barrage of sound. "I never said I'd do anything."

Vlad could see the crowd surging forward. Kill, kill, kill, the mob chanted. They were coming for him.

Now he heard shouts calling him an evil child. Evil? He wasn't evil. So what was he? Not human, not a vampire. What was it Rexus said? Neither one thing, nor the other. But that could be a good thing, couldn't it? Yes, he decided, it *was* a good thing. In spite of his pain, he wanted to scream with joy. He was neither one species nor the other. He was unique, a hupyre – the best of both. He opened his mouth and yelled.

"I AM NOT EVIL! I AM NOT EVEN A VAMPIRE. I AM A HUPYRE." He stopped and smiled at Albert Grundig. "I don't drink blood and I don't kill, but I could murder a milkshake."

"You're a hupyre? Really a hupyre? I thought they didn't exist!"

Vlad managed a smile. "That's the second time I've heard that tonight. Hupyres sure do exist."

He looked beyond Albert and saw the truck. He remembered Rexus telling him about the holy water sign in the inn. "The people queuing over there, are they filling containers with holy water?" Albert nodded. "Okay, I'll prove to you all that you have nothing to fear from me. I'll drink some holy water. Okay?"

The crowd fell silent and parted to allow Vlad through. As he got nearer to the water truck doubts filled his head. He'd figured out that none of the things to ward off evil would hurt him, because he wasn't evil. So he didn't need to fear holy water, garlic or crucifixes. But supposing he'd got it wrong? Suppose the water burnt out his insides? He looked at the faces surrounding him. All intent on watching him drink. There was no escape now. He'd have to go through with it.

Albert walked next to him and shouted out. "Petrus, pour this young hupyre a drink. We don't want any funny stuff with him pretending to pour his own, now do we?"

The crowd murmured their assent.

Vlad stopped next to the truck. He could see a face peering up at him from underneath.

"Mr Timms? What are you doing under there?"

Before Timms could answer, a man put a tankard in Vlad's hand, which shook so much he had difficulty not spilling the liquid. He raised it to his lips. It was now or never. Drink or die. If he didn't drain the lot he had no doubt the mob would lynch him and one thing was for sure, vampire, hupyre or human, a stake through the heart was deadly in every case.

He took a sip and the crowd gasped. It tasted good. He tipped the glass and drained it in one go. As the cool liquid quenched his thirst, he prayed it wouldn't suddenly turn into a raging fire.

The crowd roared with approval and several men came forward to pat him on the back and welcome him into their ranks.

"Let me through, let me through. Master Vlad, it's me, Mary."

Vlad looked up as Mary elbowed her way to the front. He handed the tankard to Albert and turned to hug her. Behind Mary came Joe, Lisette and Rexus.

"That was a brave thing you did, Vlad," said Rexus. "How did you know the water wouldn't burn you?"

"I didn't know for certain, but it was something I had to do."

"To prove to this lot you were a hupyre?" Rexus asked.

"No," Vlad said with a grin. "I did it to convince myself that I'm not evil. What's that in your hand? More holy water for me to drink?"

Rexus looked at the glass vial he held and then dropped it and crushed it with his heel. "It was something I was going to give you to drink, but I changed my mind. You don't need it now that you have an entire truckload of water next to you."

Vlad looked at the water truck. "How does the hose work on this thing?" he asked.

"We work up pressure by pumping," Petrus said. "See that contraption at the back? Two men, one on each handle, move up and down and the pressure forces the water out. Why do you want to know? Are you going to hose the castle?"

"No," said Vlad. "I have a much better idea than that. I need to find Albert."

He found Albert and took him back at the drawbridge to show him what he wanted to happen. Immediately Valentyna began yelling. Vlad was amazed to find he no longer feared her. He ignored her screeching until she mentioned his parents.

"Your parents are dead and gone, you hupyre freak. You'll never see them again."

"I don't believe you," Vlad shouted.

"You'd better believe it," she said, laughing. "I dealt with them myself. I gave each of them my personal attention. They are dead, freak boy. Dead and never coming back."

Gretchen and Boris cheered. Viktor just

smiled. Vlad felt as though he'd been hit with a brick. He'd held on to that spark of hope about his mum and dad and now it was gone. Seething with anger, he glared up at the four grinning faces. He'd been feeling bad about what he intended to do, but not any longer.

He turned to Albert. "You know what to do? Don't charge until I give the word."

Albert took the key Vlad held out and winked. Then he turned to his army.

"Come on, everyone," he shouted. "Let's get ready to root out the vampires."

Vlad went back to the water truck where men were taking it in turns to work the pump. As one fell away, exhausted, another took his place.

"There is so much pressure in there," Petrus said, "you could take the turrets off your castle when you open up the hose."

"Great," said Vlad. "Just what I need."

He took the hose and Petrus showed him how to work the valve.

"Do you want some men to help you?" Petrus asked. "The jet is going to be really strong."

"No, thank you. I want to do this myself."

"Okay, but whatever you do, hang on tight.

The force is going to knock you backwards if you don't," the fireman said.

Vlad steadied himself and focussed.

When he was ready, he yelled: "Peeeeeeeeeeeeeeeeeeaches!"

Albert heard the call. With a flourish, he turned the key in the lock. The massive gates swung open and the army surged through.

* * *

Viktor swallowed hard. "Beloved," he squeaked.

The rage in Valentyna's red eyes told him not to bother with the lovey-dovey stuff. He took a deep breath and yelled.

"Family, to the air. Retreat formation – immediately!"

Valentyna screamed as the army poured through the gates. "Tell that bleedin' weedy, puny hupyre, we'll be back! I deserve to live 'ere. I do …"

Viktor grabbed her arm and dragged her into the air. "It's time for you to be upwardly mobile, my dear."

* * *

Vlad waited until the family were airborne and then took aim. He opened the valve and the force knocked him back against the truck. Water shot in the air, showering everyone nearby. It sprayed everywhere but where he needed it. The vampires were getting away while he struggled to get the hose under control.

Suddenly the hose stopped jerking in his arms.

"I'll hold it back here, Vlad," yelled Rexus. "Get them."

Memories of Valentyna's words rang in Vlad's ears. She'd taken his parents. He wouldn't let her escape. He took aim and swung the nozzle, knocking her clean out of the sky.

Her screams disappeared as she melted, dripping into the sea below.

Vlad turned the hose on the biggest bat and Viktor ommed into watery oblivion.

Only his cousins remained and Vlad hesitated. Should he? Shouldn't he? Yeah, of course he should.

"You like playing catch," he yelled. "Catch this!"

The water cannon swung in an arc soaking both bats. They melted like butter and dripped down to join their parents floating like scum on the tide.

As the last drop fell from the sky, the crowd roared with approval.

* * *

The great hall was filled with merrymaking vampire slayers. Vlad felt the least he could do was give them a party. Without their help, he wouldn't have been able to scare his family into the air.

Albert Grundig came and sat next to Vlad.

"You do know they might come back, don't you?"

Vlad sighed. "Yes, I know. With a bit of luck the tide will scatter their bits so much it will take them a mighty long time to gather them together again."

"I'd just like to say how sorry I am that I believed your scheming aunt Elsabetta. I didn't know then what your aunt and uncle had done. But if they do come back, you only have to shout and all of us from Malign village will come to your aid."

Vlad smiled, but it was an effort. He was so tired and ached from head to toe.

Albert got up and went to join his friends. Rexus came over and sat down.

"I'll be leaving soon," said Rexus. "I'm going to walk Lisette back to Malign village and then go home to Granny."

"Would you tell her I'm sorry for leaving without saying goodbye? I was scared she'd try to stop me."

Rexus gave a short laugh. "Oh, there's no doubt about that. She would have tried to stop you."

"Rexus, did she drug my chocolate?"

Vlad waited. Rexus' mouth opened and closed, but no words came out.

"I take it that's a yes. But why?"

"Vlad," Rexus said, "I ... she ... that is, we ..."

Lisette appeared in front of them. "I'm so pleased you're all right, Vlad," she said. "Thanks to you, Mr Grundig has given me a good job at the Ye Olde Stake House. Working for your aunt Elsabetta made me miserable. I'm sure Mr Grundig will be kinder."

Vlad didn't know what to say to that, so just smiled.

"I'm ready to go back to the village now, Rexus," she said.

Rexus stood up. "Bye, Vlad. I hope to see you again one day, but don't go wandering in the forest on your own. You never know who might find you."

"You mean you won't come and visit me here? I was hoping you would," said Vlad.

"Really?" said Rexus. "You mean that? That's great. Yes, I'll come over as often as I can." He stared hard as if making up his mind about something and then he nodded. "You know that question you asked me just now? I can't answer it, but I will say this. Don't go to visit Granny, okay? Not for any reason at all."

Vlad decided he'd ask Rexus what that was all about when he didn't have Lisette with him. Although, the way they were looking at each other, he wasn't sure they'd be spending much time apart. Vlad watched them leave. Lisette looked over her shoulder and grinned at him. It was only a few days, but it seemed such a long time ago that he'd had no friends and now he had at least two.

The castle would seem very empty once everyone went home. Maybe Mary and Joe would like to move in with him. He decided to ask them later.

Mr Timms came to stand in front of Vlad and coughed.

"If you, um, would like, I'll continue to be the Malign family lawyer. I never really wanted to be a refuse collector. Shall I tell you the rhyme now? In the west wing of the tower, near to all Maligns hold dear …"

"Thank you, but I don't think I want to hear it right now," said Vlad. "Maybe tomorrow."

For tonight, all Vlad wanted was to say a quiet goodbye to his mum and dad. Even though they wouldn't be back, he knew they would always be with him. He was part of both of them. Not a vampire, not a human, but a hupyre. Something to be proud of.

The End

If you enjoyed the first Vlad the Inhaler book you might want to find out what happens next. Here is chapter one of the second Vlad book.

Vlad the Inhaler – Hero at Large

Chapter One

Vlad forced his feet to move up the stone spiral staircase of the tower's west wing. As he cupped his hand to shield the candle's flame from the draughts whistling around him, he prayed he would have the courage to go through with his quest this time. His dad would have expected him to be brave, but each time he got as far as *that* painting, he turned and ran back down the stairs, almost falling down them in his haste to get to safety.

This time, he promised himself, *this time* he would make it into the portrait gallery and find where the Malign treasure was hidden.

He repeated, over and over, the rhyme his dad had left for him.

In the west wing of the tower,
Near to all Maligns hold dear,
Full moon strikes the midnight hour
Set it right and steps appear

He'd been up here so many times, but had never yet gone beyond that terrifying first portrait. Reaching the top step, he pushed open the heavy oak door. The creaking hinges screamed into the night. He shuddered – it was loud enough to wake all his undead relatives. Taking a deep breath, he stood on the threshold of the vast hall, where hundreds of portraits of temporarily dead Maligns waited to glare down at him.

He could feel the disapproval of his ancestors radiating from the walls. How they must hate having a hupyre as heir to their vampire legacy. But the painting he needed to reach wasn't a portrait. It was of Castle Malign itself, perched high on a cliff with fearsome waves breaking on the jagged rocks far below. Opposite the painting was a tall grandfather clock, where he was sure the next clue to the treasure was hidden. Vlad loved his home, but he might not be able to keep it for much longer. If he didn't find the answer to his dad's rhymes, the castle would have to be sold to pay the mounting bills.

Timms the lawyer had made it clear that Vlad was living at the castle on borrowed time. He *had* to solve the riddle of where his dad's will was hidden – and hopefully discover piles of gold as well.

He stepped forward, trying to avoid the portrait of great-great-great grandfather Count Vincent Priceless Malign. But, as had happened every night for the last week, he could feel the long-dead count's eyes burning into him, devouring his soul. Sweat soaked through Vlad's tee-shirt as he tried to put one foot in front of the other. Don't look, he told himself. Don't even think about looking. But a much more persuasive voice whispered in his head. *Turn around, boy. Turn around and look into my eyes.*

Vlad couldn't resist, the call was too strong. He had to obey the voice. Fighting the urge to turn was useless; his body swivelled towards the portrait and his eyes focussed on his frightening ancestor. He stared at what had been painted of the Count before the artist had become Vincent's late night snack. The painter had caught the look of hunger in Vincent's eyes, but then, so legend said, Vincent had caught the artist. No more hunger and no more artist.

Find me and bring me home, boy!

Vlad shook his head, trying to block out the voice. In the portrait, Vincent clutched the necklace that had given him his name – the Priceless Pendant. All Vlad knew about the jewel was that it gave the holder whatever he or she most wanted. If Vlad owned it, he would use it to bring his parents back to life. As the thought of his mum and dad entered his head, the hold Vincent had on him seemed to weaken and Vlad was able to move away.

The verse mentioned a full moon and there was one tonight, so Vlad made himself move deeper into the gallery, until he reached the centre of the long room.

As he walked, he recited the verse once more.

In the west wing of the tower,
Near to all Maligns hold dear,
Full moon strikes the midnight hour
Set it right and steps appear

The answer had to be connected to the clock.

He walked over to it and blew out his candle so that the only illumination was the moonlight streaming in through the tower's windows. The clock was enormous, nearly three times as tall as Vlad. He concentrated on shortening his limbs, feeling the crunch as his bones contracted. His vision shifted until only pinpricks of moonlight penetrated. As he changed into bat form he shot upwards and almost collided with the ceiling. Turning into a bat was still a new skill and he found it difficult to control his movements when he first changed.

He tried to hover in front of the massive dial, but it was hard to remain still. He swooped around the gallery a few times, finally coming to land on the massive crystal chandelier hanging from the centre of the room. It was perfectly placed for Vlad to hang upside down as he studied the clock.

The seconds ticked slowly by while he clung to his precarious perch, but eventually the clock chimed midnight and ... nothing! No change. No sounds other than the chimes, no further clue and no steps!

He could have howled with frustration. What was he supposed to set right? He must be thinking about the rhyme in the wrong way.

He flew down from the chandelier and landed next to the Castle Malign painting. Stretching out his body, he resumed his human shape. No matter how many times he made the change, he was always amazed to find his clothes changed with him.

Rummaging in the pocket of his jeans, he pulled out a box of matches and relit the candle. As he headed back down the corridor towards the entrance to the staircase, the voice of Vincent Priceless Malign called out to him, but Vlad didn't stop to listen. He fled.

As he followed the spiral, winding down to the main part of the castle, he tried to think of ways to stay awake. His nightmares were getting worse each time he fell asleep and the thought of having yet another one made him feel sick. He reached the second floor and crept to the east wing, tiptoeing past his old nurse's room, so as not to wake Mary. He knew she meant well, but he wasn't a baby anymore. Sometimes he thought she'd forgotten that *he'd* saved *her* by showering Uncle Viktor and Aunt Valentyna with holy water.

He pushed open his bedroom door and peered in. Phew! No one there. He wasn't sure who he expected to see in his room, but just recently he'd felt as though the vampire relatives he'd vanquished might have found a way to come back. There was no reason for it, but try as he might, he couldn't shake off the feeling that they were out there and getting closer.

As he closed the door, shadows cast by his flickering candle painted sinister images on the walls. He forced himself not to look behind. He knew there was nothing there. He was *sure* there was nothing there. There couldn't possibly be ... he spun round to look. Hot wax flew and burned his hand. He dropped the candle and stamped on the flame before it could set fire to the rug. The clouds must have drifted away, because moonlight suddenly filled the room. Vlad picked up the trampled candle, undressed and climbed into bed without bothering to relight it.

Sitting up so that he wouldn't sleep, he sucked absentmindedly at the wax burn on his hand. Think, Vlad, think, he told himself.

In the west wing of the tower,
Near to all Maligns hold dear,
Full moon strikes the midnight hour
Set it right and steps appear

Set it right and steps appear – what did that mean? Should he take some steps up to the tower? Maybe he … What about taking the clock to pieces? He could … Stifling a massive yawn, his eyes closed and his mind drifted.

The paintings were moving. Hands reached out from the canvasses as he passed. Vlad swerved from one side of the room to the other avoiding the claws stretching out for him. Vincent Priceless Malign stepped down from his frame and towered over Vlad. The missing half of his face gradually took shape and his fangs grew.

"What's this? A disgusting half-breed hupyre? In my castle? Kill it!"

Aunt Valentyna appeared. Dripping water formed a puddle at her feet and fish splashed in it. "I'll kill the hupyre for you, Vincent."

"No," Vlad muttered, "you can't kill me. You're dead. I washed you away with holy water."

"That's what you think," Valentyna said, lunging forward with her fangs bared. The fish took flight and turned into bats.

Vlad ran, but his feet wouldn't work properly. He seemed to be wading through treacle. He could see Timms the lawyer in the far distance. If only he could reach him, maybe he'd say Vlad didn't need to solve the rhyme.

His dad appeared.

"I'm very disappointed in you, Vlad. You're going to lose the castle. The only thing all the Maligns have loved more than blood. How could you?"

"I'm trying to solve your clue, Dad. Really I am," Vlad called, but his father vanished.

He could see Timms getting further and further away, being chased by Rexus the werewolf.

"Rexus, wait for me," Vlad yelled. He missed his friend.

Then he saw Timms waving a piece of parchment and Vlad realised it was Timms he needed to reach, not Rexus. He ran towards the lawyer.

"Vlad," said Mary suddenly blocking his path, "why aren't you in bed? How many times must I tell you to stay in bed?"

Mary slowly dissolved and Valentyna took her place. "Come to me, Vlad. I'll look after you. Come and be my child."

Vlad knew she wanted to kill him, but he ran towards her. His brain screamed no, but his body hurtled into her arms. Then he looked up and his mother smiled down at him.

"Why didn't you save me, Vlad?" she asked with tears streaming down her cheeks. "I'm trapped and you haven't tried to find me. Help me, Vlad."

His dad flew above him with his arms outstretched. "We need you, Vlad. Only you can save us. Only you."

Vlad reached up for his parents, but Viktor and Valentyna took their place. Blood dripped from their fangs and splashed on Vlad's hands.

"Come along, little hupyre. Come to Uncle Viktor."

"No," screamed Vlad, but he felt himself being lifted from the ground.

Viktor took hold of Vlad and shook him. "Where is the treasure? Where is the treasure? Do you want to die?"

"No! No, I don't want to die," he yelled, then realised he'd been dreaming again.

Sweat dripped from his forehead and his palms were saturated. His heart pounded so fast he could barely breathe. He gasped, snatching at his inhaler. As the wonderful air surged back into his tortured lungs, he realised the inhaler was nearly empty.

He needed replacements, but he had no idea

where to go – or where to find the money to pay for them. He'd have to borrow the money from Mary and Joe, although they hadn't been paid for ages, just like the other staff members, so they might not have any money either.

He wedged his back into the most uncomfortable position he could find so that he wouldn't fall asleep again and put his mind to solving the rhyme.

The paintings were moving. Hands reached out from the canvasses as he passed. Vlad swerved from one side of the room to the other …

"Vlad, wake up. You're having one of your bad dreams."

He opened his eyes to find Mary holding him.

"There, there, my lambkins. Don't you fret. Mary's here."

He rested in her arms for a while, then pulled back. "Mary, I don't know what to do. I can't find Dad's will and the castle will have to be sold. I need a new inhaler and haven't a clue where to get one. The shopkeepers are demanding to be paid and I have no money.

Even Timms is threatening legal action unless I pay his bill. I feel like every time I turn around there's a new problem."

Mary sighed. "You're right, Vlad, and I'm sorry to say I've brought another one to add to your list. The maids haven't eaten since they were bitten by your aunt and uncle. They're wasting away. Unless you can think of a way to undo curse of the vampire bites, they are all going to die."

Coming soon: *Vlad the Inhaler – Hero at Large*. In addition to the *Vlad the Inhaler* trilogy, Lorraine is working on a series of novels for the same age group, featuring Jonas Fry, which could best be described as *Randall and Hopkirk (deceased)* meets *Buffy the Vampire Slayer* – but without the vampires!

Vlad's Facebook page:
https://www.facebook.com/
IamVladTheInhaler/

Lorraine's Website:
www.lorrainemace.com

Lorraine's Amazon page:
https://www.amazon.co.uk/
Lorraine-Mace/e/B002VK4UV2

Lorraine's Twitter account:
https://twitter.com/lomace

21636842R10151

Printed in Great Britain
by Amazon